GERMAN

E. T. A. Hoffmann

THE SANDMAN
THE ELEMENTARY SPIRIT

Two Mysterious Tales

MONDIAL

Mondial
New York

E. T. A. Hoffmann:
The Sandman. The Elementary Spirit
(Two Mysterious Tales)
German Classics

Translated by John Oxenford

© 2008 Mondial
(for this edition of "The Sandman. The Elementary Spirit")

Cover: *Self-Caricature*. Drawing by E. T. A. Hoffmann

ISBN 978-1-59569-117-0
Library of Congress Control Number: 2008939215

www.mondialbooks.com

THE SANDMAN

NATHANIEL TO LOTHAIRE

CERTAINLY you must all be uneasy that I have not written for so long—so very long. My mother, I am sure, is angry, and Clara will believe that I am passing my time in dissipation, entirely forgetful of the fair angel-image that is so deeply imprinted in my heart and mind. Such, however, is not the case. Daily and hourly I think of you all, and in my sweet dreams the kindly form of my lovely Clara passes before me, and smiles upon me with her bright eyes as she was wont when I appeared among you. Alas, how could I write to you in the distracted mood which has hitherto disturbed my every thought! Something horrible has crossed my path of life. Dark forebodings of a cruel, threatening, fate spread themselves over me like dark clouds, which no friendly sunbeam can penetrate. Now will I tell you what has befallen me. I must do so, that I plainly see—but if I only think of it, it will laugh out of me like mad. Ah, my dear Lothaire, how shall I begin it? How shall I make you in any way sensible that that which occurred to me a few days ago could really have such a fatal effect on my life? If you were here you could see for yourself, but now you will certainly take me for a crazy ghost-seer. In a word, the horrible thing which happened to me, and the painful impression of which I in vain endeavour to escape, is nothing more than this; that some days ago, namely on the 30th of October, at twelve o'clock at noon, a barometer-dealer came into my room and offered me his wares. I bought nothing, and threatened to throw him down stairs, upon which he took himself off of his own accord.

You suspect that only relations of the most peculiar kind, and exerting the greatest influence over my life, can give any import to this occurrence, nay, that the person of that unlucky dealer must have a hostile effect upon me. So it is, indeed. I collect myself with all my might, that patiently and quietly I may tell you so much of my early youth as will bring all plainly and clearly in bright images before your active mind. As I am about to begin I fancy that I hear you laughing and Clara saying: "Childish stories indeed!" Laugh at me I beseech you, laugh with all your heart. But, heavens, my hair stands on end, and it seems as if I am asking you to laugh at me, in mad despair, as Franz Moor asked Daniel.* But to my story.

Excepting at dinner time I and my brothers and sisters saw my father very little during the day. He was, perhaps, busily engaged at his ordinary occupation. After supper, which, according to the old custom was served up at seven o'clock, we all went with my mother into my father's workroom, and seated ourselves at the round table. My father smoked tobacco and drank a large glass of beer. Often he told us a number of wonderful stories, and grew so warm over them that his pipe continually went out. I had to light it again, with burning paper, which I thought great sport. Often, too, he would give us picture-books, and sit in his arm-chair silent and thoughtful, puffing out such thick clouds of smoke that we all seemed to be swimming in the clouds. On such evenings as these my mother was very melancholy, and immediately the clock struck nine, she would say: "Now children, to bed — to bed! The Sandman is coming, I can see." And certainly on all these occasions I heard something with a heavy, slow step go bouncing up the stairs. That I thought must be the Sandman. Once that dull noise and footstep were particularly fearful, and I asked

---

* Two characters in Schiller's play of "Die Räuber."

my mother, while she took us away: "Eh, mamma, who is this naughty Sandman, who always drives us away from papa? What does he look like?" — "There is no Sandman, dear child," replied my mother. "When I say the Sandman comes, I only mean that you are sleepy and cannot keep your eyes open, — just as if sand had been sprinkled into them." This answer of my mother's did not satisfy me — nay, in my childish mind the thought soon matured itself that she only denied the existence of the Sandman to hinder us from being terrified at him. Certainly I always heard him coming up the stairs. Full of curiosity to hear more of this Sandman, and his particular connection with children, I at last asked the old woman who tended my youngest sister what sort of man he was. "Eh, Natty," said she, "do you not know that yet? He is a wicked man, who comes to children when they will not go to bed, and throws a handful of sand into their eyes, so that they start out bleeding from their heads. These eyes he puts in a bag and carries them to the half-moon to feed his own children, who sit in the nest up yonder, and have crooked beaks like owls with which they may pick up the eyes of the naughty human children."

A most frightful image of the cruel Sandman was horribly depicted in my mind, and when in the evening I heard the noise on the stairs, I trembled with agony and alarm. My mother could get nothing out of me, but the cry of "The Sandman, the Sandman!" which was stuttered forth through my tears. I then ran into the bed-room, where the frightful apparition of the Sandman terrified me during the whole night. I had already grown old enough to perceive that the nurse's tale about the Sandman and the nest of children in the half-moon could not be quite true, but, nevertheless, this Sandman remained a fearful spectre, and I was seized with the utmost horror, when I heard him not only come up the stairs, but violently force open my father's room-door and enter. Sometimes he staid away for a long period, but often-er his visits were in close succession. This lasted for years, and I could not accustom myself to the terrible goblin; the image of the dreadful Sandman did not become more faint. His intercourse with my father began more and more to oc-cupy my fancy. An unconquerable fear prevented me from asking my father about it, but if I—I myself could penetrate the mystery, and behold the wondrous Sandman—that was the wish which grew upon me with years. The Sandman had brought me into the path of the marvellous and won-derful, which so readily finds a domicile in the mind of a child. Nothing was to me more delightful than to read or hear horrible stories of goblins, witches, pigmies, etc.; but above them all stood the Sandman, whom, in the oddest and most frightful shapes, I was always drawing with chalk or charcoal on the tables, cupboards, and walls. When I was ten years old, my mother removed me from the children's room into a little chamber, situated in a corridor near my father's room. Still, as before, we were obliged speedily to take our departure as soon as, on the stroke of nine, the unknown was heard in the house. I could hear in my little chamber how he entered my father's room, and then it soon appeared to me that a thin vapor of a singular odor dif-fused itself about the house. Stronger and stronger with my curiosity grew my resolution to form in some manner the Sandman's acquaintance. Often I sneaked from my room to the corridor, when my mother had passed, but never could I discover any thing, for the Sandman had always gone in at the door when I reached the place where I might have seen him. At last, urged by an irresistible impulse, I resolved to hide myself in my father's room and await the appearance of the Sandman.

By the silence of my father, and the melancholy of my mother, I perceived one evening that the Sandman was coming. I, therefore, feigned great weariness, left the room before nine o'clock, and hid myself in a corner close to the door. The house-door creaked, and the heavy, slow, groaning step went through the passage and towards the stairs. My mother passed me with the rest of the children. Softly — very softly, I opened the door of my father's room. He sat as usually, stiff and silent, with his back turned to the door. He did not perceive me, and I swiftly darted into the room and behind the curtain, drawn before an open press, which stood close to the door, and in which my father's clothes were hanging. The steps sounded nearer and nearer — there was a strange coughing and scraping and murmuring without. My heart trembled with anxiety and expectation. A sharp step close — very close to the door, — a smart stroke on the latch, and the door was open with a rattling noise. Screwing up my courage with all my might, I cautiously peeped out. The Sandman was standing before my father in the middle of the room, the light of the candles shone full upon his face. The Sandman, the fearful Sandman, was the old advocate Coppelius, who had often dined with us.

But the most hideous form could not have inspired me with deeper horror than this very Coppelius. Imagine a large broad-shouldered man, with a head disproportionately big, a face the colour of yellow ochre, a pair of gray bushy eyebrows, from beneath which a pair of green cat's eyes sparkled with the most penetrating lustre, and with a large nose curved over his upper lip. His wry mouth was often twisted into a malicious laugh, when a couple of dark red spots appeared upon his cheeks, and a strange hissing sound was heard through his compressed teeth. Coppelius always appeared in an ashen-gray coat, cut in old-fashioned style, with waistcoat and breeches of the same colour, while his stockings were black, and his shoes adorned with buckles set with precious stones. The little peruke scarcely reached further than the crown of his head, the curls stood high above his large red ears, and a broad hair-bag projected stiffly from his neck, so that the silver buckle which fastened his folded cravat might be plainly seen. The whole figure was hideous and repulsive, but most disgusting to us children were his coarse brown hairy fists; indeed, we did not like to eat what he had touched with them. This he had remarked, and it was his delight, under some pretext or other, to touch a piece of cake, or some nice fruit, that our kind mother might privately have put in our plate, in order that we, with tears in our eyes, might, from disgust and abhorrence, no longer be able to enjoy the treat intended for us. He acted in the same manner on holidays, when my father gave us a little glass of sweet wine. Then would he swiftly draw his fist over it, or perhaps he would even raise the glass to his blue lips, and laugh most devilishly, when we could only express our indignation by soft sobs. He always called us the little beasts, we dared not utter a sound when he was present, and we heartily cursed the ugly, unkind man, who deliberately marred our slightest pleasures. My mother seemed to hate the repulsive Coppelius as much as we did, since as soon as he showed himself her liveliness, her free and cheerful mind was changed into a gloomy solemnity. My father conducted himself towards him, as though he was a superior being, whose bad manners were to be tolerated, and who was to be kept in good humour at any rate. He need only give the slightest hint, and the favourite dishes were cooked, and the choicest wines served.

When I now saw this Coppelius, the frightful and terrific thought took possession of my soul, that indeed no one but he could be the Sandman. But the Sandman was no longer that bugbear of a nurse's tale, who provided the owl's nest in the half-moon with children's eyes, — no, he was a hideous spectral monster, who, wherever he appeared, brought with him grief, want, and destruction — temporal and eternal.

I was rivetted to the spot as if enchanted. At the risk of being discovered, and as I plainly foresaw, of being severely punished, I remained with my head peeping through the curtain. My father received Coppelius with solemnity. "Now to our work!" cried the latter with a harsh, grating voice, as he flung off his coat. My father silently and gloomily drew off his night-gown, and both attired themselves in long black frocks. Whence they took these, I did not see. My father opened the door of what I had always thought to be a cupboard, but I now saw that it was no cupboard, but rather a black hollow, in which there was a little hearth. Coppelius entered, and a blue flame began to crackle up on the hearth. All sorts of strange utensils lay around. Heavens! — As my old father now stooped down to the fire, he looked quite another man. A frightful convulsive pain seemed to have distorted his mild reverend features into a hideous repulsive diabolical countenance. He looked like Coppelius: the latter was brandishing red hot tongs, and with them taking shining masses busily out of the thick smoke, which he afterwards hammered. It seemed to me, as if I saw human faces around without any eyes — but with deep holes instead. "Eyes here, eyes!" said Coppelius in a dull roaring voice. Overcome by the wildest terror, I shrieked out, and fell from my hiding place upon the floor. Coppelius seized me, and showing his teeth, bleated out, "Ah — little wretch, — little wretch!" — then dragging me up, he flung me on the hearth, where the fire began to singe my hair. "Now we have eyes enough — a pretty pair of child's eyes." Thus whispered Coppelius and taking out of the flame some red-hot grains with his fists, he was about to sprinkle them in my eyes. My father upon this raised his hands in supplication, and cried: "Master, master, leave my Nathaniel his eyes!" Coppelius uttered a yelling laugh, and said: "Well let the lad have his eyes and cry his share in the world, but we will examine the mechanism of his hands and feet. And then he seized me so forcibly that my joints cracked, and screwed off my hands and feet, and then put them on again, one here and the other there. "Every thing is not right here! — As good as it was — the old one has understood it!" So did Coppelius say, in a hissing, lisping tone, but all around me became black and dark, a sudden cramp darted through my bones and nerves — and I lost all feeling. A gentle warm breath passed over my face; I woke as out of a sleep of death. My mother had been stooping over me. "Is the Sandman yet there?'' I stammered. "No, no, my dear child, he has gone away long ago, — he will not hurt you!" — So said my mother, and she kissed and embraced her recovered darling.

Why should I weary you, my dear Lothaire! Why should I be so diffuse with details, when I have so much more to tell. Suffice it to say, that I had been discovered while watching, and ill-used by Coppelius. Agony and terror had brought on delirium and fever, of which I lay sick for several weeks. "Is the Sandman still there?" That was my first sensible word and the sign of my amendment — my recovery. I can now only tell you, the most frightful moment in my juvenile years. Then you will be convinced that it is no fault of my eyes, that all to me seems colourless, but that a dark fatality has actually suspended over my life a gloomy veil of clouds, which I shall perhaps only tear away in death.

Coppelius was no more to be seen; it was said he had left the town.

About a year might have elapsed, when, according to the old custom, we sat at the round table. My father was very cheerful, and told much that was entertaining, about his travels in his youth; when, as the clock struck nine, we heard the house-door creak on the hinges, and slow steps, heavy as iron, groaned through the passage and up the stairs. "That is Coppelius," said my mother, turning pale. "Yes! — that is Coppelius!" repeated my father, with a faint broken voice. The tears started from my mother's eyes. "But father — father!" she cried, "must it be so?" — "He comes to me for the last time, I promise you," was the answer. "Only go now — go with the children — go — go to bed. Good night!"

I felt as if I were pressed into cold, heavy stone, — my breath was stopped. My mother caught me by the arm as I stood immoveable. "Come, come, Nathaniel!" I allowed myself to be led, and entered my chamber! "Be quiet — be quiet — go to bed — go to sleep!" cried my mother after me; but tormented by restlessness, and an inward anguish perfectly indescribable, I could not close my eyes. The hateful, abominable Coppelius stood before me with fiery eyes, and laughed at me maliciously. It was in vain that I endeavoured to get rid of his image. About midnight there was a frightful noise, like the firing of a gun. The whole house resounded. There was a rattling and a rustling by my door, and the house-door was closed with a violent sound. "That is Coppelius!" I cried, and I sprang out of bed in terror. There was then a shriek as if of acute inconsolable grief. I darted into my father's room; the door was open, a suffocating smoke rolled towards me, and the servant girl cried: "Ah, my master, my master!" On the floor of the smoking hearth lay my father dead, with his face burned and blackened, and hideously distorted, — my sisters were shrieking and moaning around him, — and my mother had fainted. "Coppelius! — cursed Satan, thou hast slain my father!" I cried, and lost my senses. When, two days afterwards, my father was laid in his coffin, his features were again as mild and gentle as they had been in his life. My soul was comforted by the thought that his compact with the devilish Coppelius could not have plunged him into eternal perdition.

The explosion had awakened the neighbours, the occurrence had become the common talk, and had reached the ears of the magistracy, who wished to make Coppelius answerable. He had, however, vanished from the spot, without leaving a trace.

If I tell you, my dear friend, that the barometer-dealer was the accursed Coppelius himself, you will not blame me for regarding a phenomenon so unpropitious as boding some heavy calamity. He was dressed differently, but the figure and features of Coppelius are too deeply imprinted in my mind, for an error in this respect to be possible. Besides, Coppelius has not even altered his name. As I hear he gives himself out as a Piedmontese optician, and calls himself Giuseppe Coppola.

I am determined to cope with him, and to avenge my father's death, be the issue what it may.

Tell my mother nothing of the hideous monster's appearance. Remember me to my dear sweet Clara, to whom I will write in a calmer mood. — Farewell.

CLARA TO NATHANIEL

It is true that you have not written to me for a long time, but nevertheless I believe that I am still in your mind and thoughts. For assuredly you were thinking of me most intently, when designing to send your last letter to my brother Lothaire, you directed it to me, instead of him. I joyfully opened the letter, and did not perceive my error till I came to the words: "Ah, my dear Lothaire." Now, by rights I should have read no farther, but should have handed over the letter to my brother. Although you have often, in your childish teasing mood, charged me with having such a quiet, womanish, steady disposition, that like the lady, even if the

house were about to fall in, I should smooth down a wrong
fold in the window curtain before I ran away, I can hardly tell you how your letter shocked me. I could scarcely
breathe,—my eyes became dizzy. Ah, my dear Nathaniel,
how could such a horrible event have crossed your life? To
be parted from you, never to see you again,—the thought
darted through my breast like a burning dagger. I read and
read. Your description of the repulsive Coppelius is terrific.
For the first time I learned how your good old father died
a shocking violent death. My brother Lothaire, to whom I
gave up the letter as his property, sought to calm me, but
in vain. The fatal barometer-maker, Giuseppe Coppola, followed me at every step, and I am almost ashamed to confess
that he disturbed my healthy and generally peaceful sleep
with all sorts of horrible visions. Yet soon,—even the next
day, I was quite changed again. Do not be offended, dearest
one, if Lothaire tells you, that in spite of your strange mis-
giving, that Coppelius will in some manner injure you, I am
in the same cheerful unembarrassed frame of mind as ever.

I will honestly confess to you that, according to my opinion, all the terrible things of which you speak, merely occurred in your own mind, and that the actual external world
had little to do with them. Old Coppelius may have been
repulsive enough, but his hatred of children was what really
caused the abhorrence of your children towards him.

In your childish mind the frightful sandman in the
nurse's tale was naturally associated with old Coppelius,
who, even if you had not believed in the sandman, would
still have been a spectral monster, especially dangerous to
children. The awful nightly occupation with your father
was no more than this, that both secretly made alchemical
experiments, and with these your mother was constantly
dissatisfied, since besides a great deal of money being use-
lessly wasted, your father's mind being filled with a falla-

cious desire after higher wisdom was alienated from his family — as they say, is always the case with such experimenalists. Your father no doubt, by some act of carelessness, occasioned his own death, of which Coppelius was completely guiltless. Would you believe it, that I yesterday asked our neighbour, the clever apothecary, whether such a sudden and fatal explosion was possible in such chemical experiments? "Certainly," he replied, and in his way told me at great length and very circumstantially how such an event might take place, uttering a number of strange-sounding names, which I am unable to recollect. Now, I know you will be angry with your Clara; you will say that her cold disposition is impenetrable to every ray of the mysterious, which often embraces man with invisible arms, that she only sees the variegated surface of the world, and has the delight of a silly child, at some gold-glittering fruit, which contains within it a deadly poison.

Ah! my dear Nathaniel! Do you not then believe that even in free, cheerful, careless minds, here may dwell the suspicion of some dread power, which endeavours to destroy us in our own selves? Forgive me, if I, a silly girl, presume in any manner to indicate, what I really think of such an internal struggle; I shall not find out the right words after all, and you will laugh at me, not because my thoughts are foolish, but because I set about so clumsily to express them.

If there is a dark power, which with such enmity and treachery lays a thread within us, by which it holds us fast, and draws us along a path of peril and destruction, which we should not otherwise have trod; if, I say, there is such a power, it must form itself within us, or from ourselves; indeed, become identical with ourselves, for it is only in this condition that we can believe in it, and want it the room which it requires, to accomplish its secret work. Now, if we have a mind, which is sufficiently firm, sufficiently strengthened by cheerful life, always to recognise this strange hostile operation as such, and calmly to follow the path which belongs to our inclination and calling, then will the dark power fail in its attempt to gain a power, that shall be a reflection of ourselves. Lothaire adds that it is certain, that the dark physical power, if of our own accord, we have yielded ourselves up to it, often draws within us some strange form, which the external world has thrown in our way, so that we ourselves kindle the spirit, which, as we in our strange delusion believe, speaks to us in that form. It is the phantom of our own selves, the close relationship with which — and its deep operation on — our mind casts us into hell, or transports us into heaven. You see, dear Nathaniel, that I and my brother Lothaire have freely given our opinion on the subject of dark powers, which subject, now I find I have not been able to write down the chief part without trouble, appears to me somewhat deep. Lothaire's last words I do not quite comprehend. I can only suspect what he means, and yet I feel as if it were all very true. I beg of you, get the ugly advocate, Coppelius, and the barometer-seller, Giuseppe Coppola, quite out of your head. Be convinced that these strange fears have no power over you, and that it is only a belief in their hostile influence that can make them hostile in reality. If the great excitement of your mind did not speak from every line of your letter, if your situation did not give me the deepest pain, I could joke about the Sandman-Advocate, and the barometer-seller, Coppelius. Be cheerful, I have determined to appear before you as your guardian-spirit, and if the ugly Coppelius takes it in his head to annoy you in your dreams, to scare him away with loud peals of laughter. I am not a bit afraid of him nor of his disgusting hands; he shall neither spoil my sweetmeats as an advocate, nor my eyes as a sandman. Ever yours, my dear Nathaniel.

Nathaniel to Lothaire

I am very sorry that in consequence of the error occasioned by my wandering state of mind, Clara broke open the letter intended for you, and read it. She has written me a very profound philosophical epistle, in which she proves, at great length, that Coppelius and Coppola only exist in my own mind, and are phantoms of myself, which will be dissipated directly I recognise them as such. Indeed, one could not believe that the mind which often peers out of those bright, smiling, childish eyes, like a sweet charming dream, could define with such intelligence, in such a professor-like manner. She appeals to you — you, it seems have been talking about me. I suppose you read her logical lectures, that she may learn to divide and sift every thing acutely. Pray leave it off. Besides it is quite certain that the barometer-dealer, Guiseppe Coppola, is not the advocate Coppelius. I attend the lectures of the professor of physics, who has lately arrived. His name is the same as that of the famous natural philosopher, Spalanzani, and he is of Italian origin. He has known Coppola for years, and moreover it is clear from his accent that he is really a Piedmontese. Coppelius was a German, but I think no honest one. Calmed I am not, and though you and Clara may consider me a gloomy visionary, I cannot get rid of the impression, which the accursed face of Coppelius makes upon me. I am glad that Coppola has left the town, as Spalanzani says. This professor is a strange fellow — a little round man, with high cheek bones, a sharp nose, pouting lips, and little piercing eyes. Yet you will get a better notion of him than by this description, if you look at the portrait of Cagliostro, designed by Chodowiecki, in one of the Berlin annuals, Spalanzani looks like that exactly. I lately went up stairs, and perceived that the curtain, which was generally drawn completely over a glass door, left a little opening on one side. I know not what curiosity impelled me to look through, a tall and very slender lady most symmetrically formed, and most splendidly attired, sat in the room by a little table on which she had laid her arms, her hands being folded together. She sat opposite to the door, so that I could completely see her angelic countenance. She did not appear to see me, and indeed there was something fixed about her eyes as if, I might almost say, she had no power of sight. It seemed to me that she was sleeping with her eyes open. I felt very uncomfortable, and therefore I slunk away into the auditorium, which was close at hand. Afterwards I learned that the form I had seen was that of Spalanzani's daughter Olympia, whom he kept confined in a very strange and improper manner, so that no one could approach her. After all, there may be something the matter with her; she is silly perhaps, or something of the kind. But why should I write you all this? I could have conveyed it better and more circumstantially by word of mouth. Know that I shall see you in a fortnight. I must again behold my dear; sweet, angelic Clara. The ill-humour will then be dispersed, which, I must confess, has endeavoured to get the mastery over me, since that fatal, sensible letter. Therefore I do not write to her to-day. A thousand greetings, etc.

* * * * *

Nothing more strange and chimerical can be imagined than that which occurred to my poor friend, the young student Nathaniel, and which I, gracious reader, have undertaken to tell you. Have you, kind reader, ever known a something that has completely filled your heart, thoughts, and senses, so as to exclude every thing else? There was in you a fermentation and a boiling, and your blood inflamed to the

hottest glow bounded through your veins, and gave a higher colour to your cheeks. Your glance was so strange, as if
you wished to perceive, in empty space, forms which to no
other eyes are visible, and your speech flowed away into
dark sighs. Then your friends asked you: "What is it, revered one?" "What is the matter, dear one." And now you
wished to express the internal picture with all its glowing
tints, with all its light and shade, and laboured hard to find
words only to begin. You thought that in the very first word
you ought to crowd together all the wonderful, noble, horrible, comical, frightful, that had happened, so that it might
strike all the hearers at once like an electric shock. But every
word, every thing that is in the form of speech, appeared to
you colourless, cold and dead. You hunt and hunt, and stut-
ter and stammer, and the sober questions of your friends
dart like icy breezes upon your internal fire until it is ready
to go out; whereas if, like a bold painter, you had first with
a few daring strokes drawn an outline of the internal picture, you might with small trouble have laid on the colours
brighter and brighter, and the living throng of various
forms would have carried your friends along with it, and
they, like you, would have seen themselves in the picture
that had proceeded from your mind. Now I must confess
to you, kind reader, that no one has really asked me for the
history of the young Nathaniel, but you know well enough
that I belong to the queer race of authors, who, if they have
any thing in their mind, such as I have just described, feel
as if every one who comes near them, and indeed perhaps
the whole world besides, is asking them: "What is it then —
tell it, my dear friend?" Thus was I forcibly compelled to
tell you of the momentous life of Nathaniel. The singularity
and marvellousness of the story filled my entire soul, but
for that very reason and because, my reader, I had to make
you equally inclined to endure oddity, which is no small

matter, I tormented myself to begin the history of Nathaniel in a manner as inspiring, original and striking as possible. "Once upon a time," the beautiful beginning of every tale, was too tame. "In the little provincial town of S— lived" — was somewhat better, as it at least prepared for the climax. Or should I dart at once *medias in res,* with "Go to the devil, cried the student Nathaniel with rage and horror in his wild looks, when the barometer-seller, Guiseppe Coppola...?" — I had indeed already written this down, when I fancied that in the wild looks of the student Nathaniel, I could detect something ludicrous, whereas the story is not comical at all. No form of language suggested itself to my mind, which even in the slightest degree seemed to reflect the colouring of the internal picture. I resolved that I would not begin it at all. So take, gentle reader, the three letters, which friend Lothaire was good enough to give me, as the sketch of the picture which I shall endeavour to colour more and more as I proceed in my narrative. Perhaps, like a good portrait-painter, I may succeed in catching many a form in such a manner, that you will find it is a likeness without having the original, and feel as if you had often seen the person with your own corporeal eyes. Perchance, dear reader, you will then believe that nothing is stranger and madder than actual life, and that this is all that the poet can conceive, as it were in the dull reflection of a dimly polished mirror.

In order that that which it is necessary in the first place to know, may be made clearer, we must add to these letters the circumstance, that shortly after the death of Nathaniel's father, Clara and Lothaire, the children of a distant relative, who had likewise died, and left them orphans, were taken by Nathaniel's mother to her own home. Clara and Nathaniel formed a strong attachment for each other, and no one in the world having any objection to make, they were betrothed, when Nathaniel left the place to pursue his studies in G—. He is, according to the date of his last letter, hearing the lectures of the celebrated professor of physics, Spalanzani.

Now I could proceed in my story with confidence, but at this moment Clara's image stands so plainly before me, that I cannot look another way, as indeed was always the case when she gazed at me, with one of her lively smiles. Clara could not by any means be reckoned beautiful; that was the opinion of all who are competent judges of beauty, by their calling. Nevertheless, the architects praised the exact symmetry of her frame, and the painters considered her neck, shoulders, and bosom almost too chastely formed, but then they all fell in love with her wondrous Magdalen-hair, and above every thing prated about *battonisch* colouring. One of them, a most fantastical fellow, singularly compared Clara's eyes to a lake by Ruysdael, in which the pure azure of a cloudless sky, the wood and flowery field, the whole cheerful life of the rich landscape are reflected. Poets and composers went still further. "What is a lake—what is a mirror!" said they, "can we look upon the girl without wondrous, heavenly songs and tunes flashing towards us from her glances, and penetrating our inmost soul, so that all there is awakened and stirred. If even then we sing nothing that is really sensible, there is not much in us, and that we can feelingly read in the delicate smile which plays on Clara's lips, when we presume to tinkle something before her, which is to pass for a song, although it is only a confused jumble of tones." So it was. Clara had the vivid fancy of a cheerful, unembarrassed child, a deep, tender, feminine disposition, an acute, clever understanding. The misty dreams had but a bad chance with her, since, though she did not talk,—as indeed talking would have been altogether repugnant to her tacit nature, her bright glance and her firm ironical smile would say to them: "Good friends, how can you imagine that I shall take your fleeting shadowy images for real forms with life and motion?" On this account Clara was censured by many as cold, unfeeling and prosaic; while others, who conceived life in its clear depth, greatly loved the feeling, acute, childlike girl, but none so much as Nathaniel, whose perception in art and science was clear and strong. Clara was attached to her lover with all her soul, and when he parted from her, the first cloud passed over her life. With what transport did she rush into his arms when, as he had promised in his last letter to Lothaire, he had actually returned to his native town and entered his mother's room. Nathaniel's expectations were completely fulfilled; for directly he saw Clara he thought neither of the Advocate Coppelius, nor of her "sensible" letter. All gloomy forebodings had gone.

However, Nathaniel was quite right, when he wrote to his friend Lothaire that the form of the repulsive barometer-seller, Coppola, had had a most hostile effect on his life. All felt, even in the first days, that Nathaniel had undergone a thorough change in his whole temperament. He sank into a gloomy reverie, and conducted himself in a strange manner, that had never been known in him before. Every thing, his whole life, had become to him a dream and a foreboding, and he was always saying that every man, although he might think himself free, only served for the cruel sport of dark powers. These he said it was vain to resist, and man must patiently resign himself to his fate. He went even so far as to say, that it is foolish to think that we do any thing in art and science according to our own self-acting will, for the inspiration which alone enables us to produce any thing, does not proceed from within ourselves, but is the effect of a higher principle without.

To the clear-headed Clara this mysticism was in the highest degree repugnant, but contradiction appeared to be useless. Only when Nathaniel proved that Coppelius was the evil principle, which had seized him at the moment when he was listening behind the curtain, and that this repugnant principle would in some horrible manner disturb the happiness of their life, Clara grew very serious, and said: "Yes, Nathaniel, you are right. Coppelius is an evil, hostile principle; he can produce terrible effects, like a diabolical power that has come invisibly into life; but only then, when you will not banish him from your mind and thoughts. So long as you believe in him he really exists, and exerts his influence; only your belief is his power."

Nathaniel, quite indignant that Clara established the demon's existence only in his own mind, would then come out with all the mystical doctrine of devils and fearful powers. But Clara would break off peevishly, by introducing some indifferent matter, to the no small annoyance of Nathaniel. He thought that such deep secrets were closed to cold, unsusceptible minds, without being clearly aware that he reckoned Clara among these subordinate natures, and therefore he constantly endeavoured to initiate her into the mysteries. In the morning, when Clara was getting breakfast ready, he stood by her, and read out of all sorts of mystical books, till she cried: "But, dear Nathaniel, suppose I blame you as the evil principle, that has a hostile effect upon my coffee? For if to please you, I leave every thing standing still, and look in your eyes, while you read, my coffee will run into the fire, and none of you will get any breakfast."

Nathaniel closed the book at once, and hurried indignantly to his chamber. Once he had a remarkable *forte* for graceful, lively tales, which he wrote down, and to which Clara listened with the greatest delight; now, his creations were gloomy, incomprehensible, formless, so that although Clara, out of compassion, did not say so, he plainly felt how little she was interested. Nothing was more insupportable to Clara than tediousness; in her looks and in her words a mental drowsiness, not to be conquered, was expressed. Nathaniel's productions were, indeed, very tedious. His indignation at Clara's cold, prosaic disposition constantly increased, and Clara could not overcome her dislike of Nathaniel's dark, gloomy, tedious mysticism, so that they became more and more estranged from each other in mind, without perceiving it. The form of the ugly Coppelius, as Nathaniel himself was forced to confess, grew more dim in his fancy, and it often cost him trouble to colour with sufficient liveliness in his pictures, when he appeared as a ghastly bugbear of fate. At last it struck him that he would make the gloomy foreboding, that Coppelius would destroy his happiness in love, the subject of a poem. He represented himself and Clara as united by true love; but occasionally it seemed as though a black hand darted into their life, and tore away some newly-springing joy. At last, while they were standing at the altar, the hideous Coppelius appeared, and touched Clara's lively eyes. They flashed into Nathaniel's heart, like bleeding sparks, scorching and burning, when Coppelius caught him, and flung him into a flaming, fiery circle, which flew round with the swiftness of the stream, and carried him along with it, amid its roaring. The roar is like that of the hurricane, when it fiercely lashes the foaming waves, which, like black giants with white heads, rise up for the furious combat. But through the wild tumult he hears Clara's voice: "Can you not, then, see me? Coppelius has deceived you. Those, indeed, were not my eyes, which so burned in your breast — they were glowing drops of your own heart's blood. I have my eyes still — only look at them!" Nathaniel reflects: "That is Clara, and I am hers for ever!" Then it seems to him as though thought forcibly entered the fiery circle, which stands still, while the noise dully ceases in the dark abyss. Nathaniel looks into Clara's eyes, but it is only death that, with Clara's eyes, kindly looks on him.

While Nathaniel composed this poem he was very calm and collected; he polished and improved every line, and having subjected himself to the fetters of metre, he did not rest till all was correct and melodious. When at last he had finished and read the poem aloud to himself, a wild horror seized him, and he cried out: "Whose horrible voice is that?" Soon, however, the whole appeared to him a very successful work, and he felt that it must inflame Clara's cold temperament, although he did not clearly consider for what Clara was to be excited, nor what purpose it would answer to torment her with the frightful images which threatened a horrible destiny, destructive to their love. Both of them—that is to say Nathaniel and Clara—were sitting in their mother's little garden, Clara very cheerful, because Nathaniel, during the three days in which he had been writing his poem, had not teased her with his dreams and his forebodings. Even Nathaniel spoke lively and joyfully about pleasant matters, as he used to do formerly, so that Clara said: "Now for the first time I have you again! Do you not see that we have driven away the ugly Coppelius?" Then it first struck Nathaniel that he had in his pocket the poem, which he had intended to read. He at once drew the sheets out and began, while Clara, expecting something tedious as usual, resigned herself and began quietly to knit. But as the dark cloud rose ever blacker and blacker, she let the stocking fall and looked full into his face. He was carried along unceasingly by his poem, an internal fire deeply reddened his cheeks, tears flowed from his eyes. At last when he had concluded, he groaned in a state of utter exhaustion, and catching Clara's hand, sighed forth, as if melted into the most inconsolable grief: "Oh Clara!—Clara!" Clara pressed him gently to her bosom, and said softly, but very solemnly and sincerely: "Nathaniel, dearest Nathaniel, do throw that mad, senseless, insane stuff into the fire!" Upon this Nathaniel sprang up enraged, and thrusting Clara from him, cried: "Thou inanimate, accursed automaton!" He ran off; Clara, deeply offended, shed bitter tears, and sobbed aloud: "Ah, he has never loved me, for he does not understand me." Lothaire entered the arbour; Clara was obliged to tell him all that had occurred. He loved his sister with all his soul, and every word of her complaint fell like a spark of fire into his heart, so that the indignation which he had long harboured against the visionary Nathaniel, now broke out into the wildest rage. He ran to Nathaniel and reproached him for his senseless conduct towards his beloved sister in hard words, which the infuriated Nathaniel retorted in the same style. The appellation of "fantastical, mad fool," was answered by that of "miserable common-place fellow." A duel was inevitable. They agreed on the following morning, according to the academical custom of the place, to fight with sharp rapiers behind the garden. Silently and gloomily they slunk about. Clara had overheard the violent dispute, and seeing the fencing-master bring the rapiers at dawn, guessed what was to occur. Having reached the place of combat, Lothaire and Nathaniel had in gloomy silence flung off their coats, and with the fierce desire of fighting in their flaming eyes, were about to fall upon one another, when Clara rushed through the garden door. Sobbing, she cried aloud, "Ye wild cruel men! Strike me down before you attack each other, for how shall I live longer in the world if my lover murders my brother, or my brother murders my lover." Lothaire lowered his weapon, and looked in silence on the ground; but in Nathaniel's heart, amid the most poignant sorrow, revived all the love for the beautiful Clara, which he had felt in the best days of his happy youth. The weapon fell from his hand, he threw himself at Clara's feet. "Can you ever forgive me, my only — my beloved Clara? Can you forgive me, my dear brother, Lothaire?"

E. T. A. HOFFMANN

Lothaire was touched by the deep contrition of his friend; all three embraced in reconciliation amid a thousand tears, and vowed eternal love and fidelity.

Nathaniel felt as though a heavy burden, which pressed him to the ground, had been rolled away, as though by resisting the dark power, which held him fast, he had saved his whole being, which had been threatened with annihilation. Three happy days he passed with his dear friends, and then went to G—, where he intended to stay a year, and then to return to his native town for ever.

All that referred to Coppelius was kept a secret from the mother, for it was well known that she could not think of him without terror, as she, as well as Nathaniel, accused him of causing her husband's death.

* * * * *

How surprised was Nathaniel, when proceeding to his lodging, he saw that the whole house was burned down, and that only the bare walls stood up amid the ashes. However, notwithstanding the fire had broken out in the laboratory of the apothecary who lived on the ground-floor, and had therefore consumed the house from bottom to top, some bold active friends had succeeded in entering Nathaniel's room in the upper story, in time to save the books, manuscripts, and instruments. They carried all safe and sound into another house, where they took a room, which Nathaniel entered at once. He did not think it at all remarkable that he lodged opposite to Professor Spalanzani; neither did it appear singular when he perceived that his window looked straight into the room where Olympia often sat alone, so that he could plainly recognise her figure, although the features of her face were indistinct and confused. At last

it struck him, that Olympia often remained for hours in
this attitude, in which he had once seen her through the
glass-door, sitting at a little table without any occupation,
and that she plainly enough looked over at him with an un-
varying glance. He was forced to confess that he had never
seen a more lovely form, but with Clara in his heart, the stiff
Olympia was perfectly indifferent to him. Occasionally, to
be sure, he gave a transient look over his compendium, at
the beautiful statue, but that was all. He was just writing to
Clara, when he heard a light tap at the door; it paused at his
words, and the repulsive face of Coppola peeped in. Nathaniel's heart trembled within him, but remembering what
Spalanzani had told him about the countryman, Coppola,
and also the sacred promises he had made to Clara with
respect to the Sandman Coppelius, he felt ashamed of his
childish fear, and collecting himself with all his might, said
as softly and civily as possible: "I do not want a barometer,
my good friend; pray, go." Upon this, Coppola advanced a
good way into the room, and said in a hoarse voice, while
his wide mouth distorted itself into a hideous laugh, and
his little eyes under their long gray lashes sparkled forth
piercingly: "Eh, eh—no barometer—no barometer? I have
besides pretty eyes— pretty eyes!" —"Madman!" cried Nathaniel with horror, "how can you have eyes?—Eyes?" But
Coppola had already put his barometer aside, and plunged
his hand into his wide coat-pocket, whence he drew lunettes
and spectacles, which he placed upon the table "There—
there—spectacles on the nose, those are my eyes—pretty
eyes!" And so saying he drew out more and more spectacles
so that the whole table began to glisten and sparkle in the
most extraordinary manner. A thousand eyes glanced, and
quivered convulsively, and stared at Nathaniel; yet he could
not look away from the table, and Coppola kept still lay-
ing down more and more spectacles, while flaming glances

were intermingled more and more wildly, and shot their blood-red rays into Nathaniel's breast. Overcome with horror, he shrieked out: "Hold, hold, frightful man!" He seized fast by the arm Coppola, who was searching his pockets to bring out still more spectacles, although the whole table was already covered. Coppola had greatly extricated himself with a hoarse repulsive laugh, and with the words "Ah, nothing for you—but here are pretty glasses" he had collected all the spectacles, put them up, and from the breast-pocket of his coat had drawn forth a number of telescopes large and small. As soon as the spectacles were removed Nathaniel felt quite easy, and thinking of Clara, perceived that the hideous phantom was but the creature of his own mind, and that Coppola was an honest optician, and could by no means be the accursed double of Coppelius. Moreover, in all the glasses which Coppola now placed on the table, there was nothing remarkable, or at least nothing so ghost-like as the spectacles, and to make matters right Nathaniel resolved to buy something of Coppola. He took up a little and very neatly worked pocket-telescope, and looked through the window to try it. Never in his life had he met a glass which brought the objects so sharply, plainly, and clearly before his eyes. Involuntarily he looked into Spalanzani's room; Olympia was sitting as usual before the little table, with her arms laid upon it, and her hands folded. For the first time could he see the wondrous beauty in the form of her face;—only the eyes seemed to him singularly stiff and dead. Nevertheless, as he looked more sharply through the glass, it seemed to him as if moist morn-beams were rising in the eyes of Olympia. It was as if the power of seeing was kindled for the first time; the glances flashed with constantly increasing liveliness. As if spell-bound, Nathaniel reclined against the window, meditating on the charming Olympia. A hemming and scraping aroused him as if from a dream. Coppola was standing behind him: "*Tre zecchini* — three ducats!" Nathaniel, who had quite forgotten the optician, quickly paid him what he asked. "Is it not so? A pretty glass — a pretty glass?" asked Coppola, in his hoarse, repulsive voice, and with his malicious smile. "Yes — yes," replied Nathaniel, peevishly; "good bye, friend." Coppola left the room, not without casting many strange glances at Nathaniel. He heard him laugh loudly on the stairs. "Ah," thought Nathaniel, "he is laughing at me because no doubt, I have paid him too much for this little glass." While he softly uttered these words, it seemed as if a deep deadly sigh was sounding fearfully through the room, and his breath was stopped by inward anguish. He perceived, however, that it was himself that had sighed. "Clara," he said to himself, "is right in taking me for a senseless dreamer, but it is pure madness — nay, more than madness, that the stupid thought, that I have paid Coppola too much for the glass, pains me even so strangely. I cannot see the cause." He now sat down to finish his letter to Clara; but a glance through the window convinced him that Olympia was still sitting there, and he instantly sprang out, as if impelled by an irresistible power, seized Coppola's glass, and could not tear himself from the seductive view of Olympia, till his friend and brother Sigismund called him to go to Professor Spalanzani's lecture. The curtain was drawn close before the fatal room, and he could neither perceive Olympia now nor during the two following days, although he scarcely ever left the window, and constantly looked through Coppola's glass. On the third day the windows were completely covered. Quite in despair, and impelled by a burning wish, he ran out of the town-gate. Olympia's form floated before him in the air, stepped forth from the bushes, and peeped at him with large beaming eyes from the clear brook. Clara's image had completely vanished from his mind; he thought of nothing but Olympia, and complained aloud and in a murmuring tone: "Ah, thou noble, sublime star of my love, hast thou only risen upon me, to vanish immediately, and leave me in dark hopeless night?"

When he was retiring to his lodging, he perceived that there was a great bustle in Spalanzani's house. The doors were wide open, all sorts of utensils were being carried in, the windows of the first floor were being taken out, maid servants were going about sweeping and dusting with great hair-brooms, and carpenters and upholsterers were knocking and hammering within. Nathaniel remained standing in the street in a state of perfect wonder, when Sigismund came up to him, laughing, and said: "Now, what do you say to our old Spalanzani?" Nathaniel assured him that he could say nothing because he knew nothing about the professor, but on the contrary perceived with astonishment the mad proceedings in a house otherwise so quiet and gloomy. He then learnt from Sigismund that Spalanzani intended to give a grand festival on the following day, — a concert and ball — and that half the university was invited. It was generally reported that Spalanzani, who had so long kept his daughter most painfully from every human eye, would now let her appear for the first time.

Nathaniel found a card of invitation, and with heart beating highly went at the appointed hour to the professor's, where the coaches were already rolling, and the lights were shining in the decorated saloons. The company was numerous and brilliant. Olympia appeared dressed with great richness and taste. Her beautifully turned face, her figure called for admiration. The somewhat strange bend of her back inwards, the wasp-like thinness of her waist, seemed to be produced by too tight lacing. In her step and deportment there was something measured and stiff, which struck many as unpleasant, but it was ascribed to

the constraint produced by the company. The concert began. Olympia played the piano with, great dexterity, and
executed a bravura, with a voice, like the sound of a glass
bell, clear, and almost cutting. Nathaniel was quite enrap-
tured; he stood in the hindermost row, and could not perfectly recognise Olympia's features in the dazzling light.
He, therefore, quite unperceived, took out Coppola's glass,
and looked towards the fair Olympia. Ah! then he saw,
with what a longing glance she looked towards him, how
every tone first resolved itself plainly in the glance of love,
which penetrated, in its glowing career, his inmost soul.
The artistical *roulades* seemed to Nathaniel the exultation
of a mind illuminated with love, and when, at last, after the
cadence, the long trill sounded shrilly through the saloon,
he felt as if grasped by glowing arms; he could no longer re-
strain himself, but with mingled pain and rapture shouted
out, "Olympia!" All looked at him, and many laughed. The
organist of the cathedral made a more gloomy face than
usual, and simply said: "Well, well." The concert had finished, the ball began. "To dance with her — with her!" That
was the aim of all Nathaniel's wishes, of all his efforts; but
how to gain courage to ask her, the queen of the festival?
Nevertheless — he himself did not know how it happened —
no sooner had the dancing begun, than he was standing
close to Olympia, who had not yet been asked to dance,
and, scarcely able to stammer out a few words, had seized
her hand. The hand of Olympia was as cold as ice; he felt a
horrible deadly frost thrilling through him. Ho looked into
her eye — that was beaming full of love and desire, and at
the same time it seemed as though the pulse began to beat,
and the stream of life to glow in the cold hand. And in the
soul of Nathaniel the joy of love rose still higher; he clasped
the beautiful Olympia, and with her flew through the
dance. He thought that his dancing was usually correct as

to time, but the peculiar rhythmical steadiness with which Olympia moved, and which often put him completely out, soon showed him, that his time was very defective. However, he would dance with no other lady, and would have liked to murder any one who approached Olympia for the purpose of asking her. But this only happened twice, and to his astonishment Olympia remained seated after every dance, when he lost no time in making her rise again. Had he been able to see any other object besides the fair Olympia, all sorts of unfortunate quarrels would have been inevitable, for the half-soft, scarcely-suppressed laughter, which arose among the young people in every corner, was manifestly directed to Olympia, whom they pursued with very curious glances—one could not tell why. Heated by the dance, and by the wine, of which he had freely partaken, Nathaniel had laid aside all his ordinary reserve. He sat by Olympia, with her hand in his, and, highly inflamed and inspired, told his passion, in words which no one understood—neither himself nor Olympia. Yet, perhaps, *she* did; for she looked immoveably in his face, and sighed several times, "Ah, ah!" Upon this, Nathaniel said, "Oh, thou splendid, heavenly lady! Thou ray from the promised land of love—thou deep soul, in which all my being is reflected!" with much more stuff of the like kind; but Olympia merely went on sighing, "Ah—ah!" Professor Spalanzani occasionally passed the happy pair, and smiled on them, with a look of singular satisfaction. To Nathaniel, although he felt in quite another region, it seemed all at once as though Professor Spalanzani was glowing considerably darker; he looked around, and, to his no small horror, perceived that the two last candles in the empty saloon had burned down to their sockets, and were just going out. Music and dancing had ceased long ago. "Separation—separation!" he cried, wildly, and in despair; he kissed Olympia's hand, he bent towards her mouth, when his glowing lips were met by lips cold as ice! Just as when he touched Olympia's cold hand, he felt himself overcome by horror; the legend of the dead bride darted suddenly through his mind, but Olympia pressed him fast, and her lips seemed to recover to life at his kiss. Professor Spalanzani strode through the empty hall, his steps caused a hollow echo, and his figure, round which a flickering shadow played, had a fearful, spectral appearance. "Dost thou love me, dost thou love me, Olympia? Only this word! — Dost thou love me?" So whispered Nathaniel; but Olympia, as she rose, only sighed, "Ah — ah!" — "Yes, my gracious, my beautiful star of love," said Nathaniel, "thou hast risen upon me, and thou wilt shine, ever illuminating my inmost soul." "Ah — ah!" replied Olympia, going. Nathaniel followed her; they both stood before the professor.

"You have had a very animated conversation with my daughter," said he, smiling; "so; dear Herr Nathaniel, if you have any taste for talking with a silly girl, your visits shall be welcome."

Nathaniel departed, with a whole heaven beaming in his bosom. The next day Spalanzani's festival was the subject of conversation. Notwithstanding the professor had done every thing to appear splendid, the wags had all sorts of incongruities and oddities to talk about, and were particularly hard upon the dumb, stiff Olympia, to whom, in spite of her beautiful exterior, they ascribed absolute stupidity, and were pleased to find therein the cause why Spalanzani kept her so long concealed. Nathaniel did not hear this without increased rage; but, nevertheless, he held his peace, for, thought he, "Is it worth while to convince these fellows that it is their own stupidity that prevents them from recognising Olympia's deep, noble mind?"

One day Sigismund said to him: "Be kind enough, brother, to tell me how it was possible for a sensible fellow like you to fall in love with that wax face, that wooden doll up there?"

Nathaniel was about to fly out in a passion, but he quickly recollected himself, and retorted: "Tell me, Sigismund, how it is that Olympia's heavenly charms could escape your glance, which generally perceives every thing so clearly—your active senses? But, for that very reason, Heaven be thanked, I have not you for my rival; otherwise, one of us must have fallen a bleeding corpse!"

Sigismund plainly perceived his friend's condition, so he skilfully gave the conversation a turn, and added, after observing that in love-affairs there was no disputing about the object: "Nevertheless it is strange, that many of us think much the same about Olympia. To us—pray do not take it ill, brother,—she appears singularly stiff and soulless. Her shape is symmetrical—so is her face—that is true! She might pass for beautiful, if her glance were not so utterly without a ray of life—without the power of seeing. Her pace is strangely measured, every movement seems to depend on some wound-up clockwork. Her playing—her singing has the unpleasantly correct and spiritless measure of a singing machine, and the same may be said of her dancing. To us, this Olympia has been quite unpleasant; we wished to have nothing to do with her; it seems as if she acts like a living being, and yet has some strange peculiarity of her own." Nathaniel did not completely yield to the bitter feeling, which was coming over him at these words of Sigismund; he mastered his indignation, and merely said, with great earnestness, "Well may Olympia appear awful to you, cold prosaic man. Only to the poetical mind does the similarly organised develop itself. To me alone was her glance of love revealed, beaming through mind and thought; only in the love of Olympia do I find myself again. It may not suit you, that she does not indulge in idle chit-chat like other shallow minds. She utters few words, it is true, but these few words appear as genuine hieroglyphics of the inner world, full of love and deep knowledge of the spiritual life in contemplation of the eternal *yonder*. But you have no sense for all this, and my words are wasted on you." — "God preserve you, brother," said Sigismund very mildly, almost sorrowfully; "but it seems to me, that you are in an evil way. You may depend upon me, if all — no, no, I will not say any thing further." All of a sudden it seemed to Nathaniel as if the cold prosaic Sigismund meant very well towards him, and, therefore, he shook the proffered hand very heartily.

Nathaniel had totally forgotten, that there was in the world a Clara, whom he had once loved; — his mother — Lothaire — all had vanished from his memory; he lived only for Olympia, with whom he sat for hours every day, uttering strange fantastical stuff about his love, about the sympathy that glowed to life, about the affinity of souls, to all of which Olympia listened with great devotion. From the very bottom of his desk, he drew out all that he had ever written. Poems, fantasies, visions, romances, tales — this stock was daily increased with all sorts of extravagant sonnets, stanzas, and *canzone,* and he read all to Olympia for hours in succession without fatigue. Never had he known such an admirable listener. She neither embroidered nor knitted, she never looked out of window, she fed no favourite bird, she played neither with lap-dog nor pet cat, she did not twist a slip of paper nor any thing else in her hand, she was not obliged to suppress a yawn by a gentle forced cough. In short, she sat for hours, looking straight into her lover's eyes, without stirring, and her glance became more and more lively and animated. Only when Nathaniel rose at last, and kissed her hand and also her lips, she said "Ah, ah!" adding "good night, dearest!" — "Oh deep, noble mind!" cried Nathaniel in his own room, "by thee, by thee, dear one, am

I fully comprehended." He trembled with inward transport, when he considered the wonderful accordance that was revealed more and more every day in his own mind, and that of Olympia, for it seemed to him as if Olympia had spoken concerning him and his poetical talent out of the depths of his own mind;—as if the voice had actually sounded from within himself. That must indeed have been the case, for Olympia never uttered any words whatever beyond those which have been already mentioned. Even when Nathaniel, in clear and sober moments, as for instance, when he had just woke in the morning, remembered Olympia's utter passivity, and her paucity and scarcity of words, he said: "Words, words! The glance of her heavenly eye speaks more than any language here below. Can a child of heaven adapt herself to the narrow circle which a miserable earthly necessity has drawn?" Professor Spalanzani appeared highly delighted at the intimacy of his daughter with Nathaniel. To the latter he gave the most unequivocal signs of approbation, and when Nathaniel ventured at last to hint at an union with Olympia, he smiled with his white face, and thought "he would leave his daughter a free choice in the matter." Encouraged by these words, and with burning passion in his heart, Nathaniel resolved to implore Olympia on the very next day, that she would say directly, in plain words, that which her kind glance had told him long ago; namely, that she loved him. He sought the ring which his mother had given him at parting, that he might give it to Olympia as a symbol of his devotion, of his life which budded forth and bloomed with her alone. Clara's letters and Lothaire's came into his hands during the search; but he flung them aside indifferently, found the ring, put it up and hastened over to Olympia. Already on the steps, in the hall he heard a strange noise, which seemed to proceed from Spalanzani's room. There was a stamping, a clattering, a pushing, a hurling against the door, intermingled with curses and imprecations. "Let go, let go, rascal!—scoundrel! Body and soul ventured in it? Ha, ha, ha! that I never will consent to—I, I made the eyes, I the clockwork—stupid blockhead with your clockwork—accursed dog of a bungling watchmaker—off with you—Satan—stop, pipe-maker—infernal beast—hold—begone—let go!" These words were uttered by the voices of Spalanzani, and the hideous Coppelius, who was thus raging and clamoring. Nathaniel rushed in, overcome by the most inexpressible anguish. The professor held a female figure fast by the shoulders, the Italian Coppola grasped it by the feet, and thus they were tugging and pulling, this way and that, contending for the possession of it, with the unmost fury. Nathaniel started back with horror, when in the figure he recognised Olympia. Boiling with the wildest indignation, he was about to rescue his beloved from these infuriated men, but at that moment, Coppola, turning himself with the force of a giant, wrenched the figure from the professor's hand, and then with the figure itself gave him a tremendous blow, which made him reel and fall backwards over the table, where vials, retorts, bottles, and glass cylinders were standing. All these were dashed to a thousand shivers. Now Coppola flung the figure across his shoulders, and, with frightful, yelling laughter, dashed down the stairs, so that the feet of the figure, which dangled in the ugliest manner, rattled with a wooden sound on every step. Nathaniel stood paralysed; he had seen but too plainly that Olympia's waxen, deadly pale countenance had no eyes, but black holes instead—she was, indeed, a lifeless doll. Spalanzani was writhing on the floor; the pieces of glass had cut his head, heart, and arms, and the blood was spirting up, as from so many fountains. But he soon collected all his strength. "After him—after him—why do you pause? Coppelius, Coppelius, has robbed me of my best automaton—a work of twenty years—body and soul set upon it—the clock-work—the speech—the walk, mine; the eyes stolen from you. The infernal rascal—after him; fetch Olympia—there you have the eyes!"

And now Nathaniel saw how a pair of eyes, which lay upon the ground, were staring at him; these Spalanzani caught up, with the unwounded hand, and flung against his heart. At this, madness seized him with its burning claws, and clutched into his soul, tearing to pieces all his thoughts and senses. "Ho—ho—ho—a circle of fire! of fire!—turn thyself round, circle! merrily, merrily, ho, thou wooden doll—turn thyself, pretty doll!" With these words he flew at the professor and pressed in his throat. He would have strangled him, had not the noise attracted many people, who rushed in, forced open Nathaniel's grasp, and thus saved the professor, whose wounds were bound immediately. Sigismund, strong as he was, was not able to master the mad Nathaniel, who with frightful voice kept crying out: "Turn thyself, wooden doll!" and struck around him with clenched fists. At last the combined force of many succeeded in overcoming him, in flinging him to the ground, and binding him. His words were merged into a hideous roar, like that of a brute, and raging in this insane condition he was taken to the mad-house.

Before, gentle reader, I proceed to tell thee what more befell the unfortunate Nathaniel, I can tell thee, in case thou takest an interest in the skilful optician and automaton-maker, Spalanzani, that he was completely healed of his wounds. He was, however, obliged to leave the university, because Nathaniel's story had created a sensation, and it was universally deemed an unpardonable imposition to smuggle wooden dolls instead of living persons into respectable tea-parties—for such Olympia had visited with success. The lawyers called it a most subtle deception, and the more culpable, inasmuch as he had planned it so artfully against the public, that not a single soul—a few cunning students excepted—had detected it, although all now wished to play the acute, and referred to various facts, which appeared to them suspicious. Nothing very clever was revealed in this way. For instance, could it strike any one as so very suspicious, that Olympia, according to the expression of an elegant tea-ite, had, contrary to all usage, sneezed oftener than she had yawned? "The *former*" remarked this elegant person, "was the self-winding-up of the concealed clockwork, which had, moreover, creaked audibly"— and so on. The professor of poetry and eloquence took a pinch of snuff, clapped first the lid of his box, cleared his throat, and said, solemnly, "Ladies and gentlemen, do you not perceive how the whole affair lies? It is all an allegory—a continued metaphor—you understand me—*Sapienti sat.*" But many were not satisfied with this; the story of the automaton had struck deep root into their souls, and, in fact, an abominable mistrust against human figures in general, began to creep in. Many lovers, to be quite convinced that they were not enamoured of wooden dolls, would request their mistress to sing and dance a little out of time, to embroider and knit, and play with their lap-dogs, while listening to reading, etc.; and, above all, not to listen merely, but also sometimes to talk, in such a manner as presupposed actual thought and feeling. With many did the bond of love become firmer, and more chaining, while others, on the contrary, slipped gently out of the noose. "One cannot really answer for this," said some. At tea-parties, yawning prevailed to an incredible extent, and there was no sneezing at all, that all suspicion might be avoided. Spalanzani, as already stated, was obliged to decamp, to escape the criminal prosecution for fraudulently introducing an automaton into human society. Coppola had vanished also.

Nathaniel awakened as from a heavy, frightful dream; he opened his eyes, and felt an indescribable sensation of pleasure streaming through him, with soft heavenly warmth. He was in bed in his own room, in his father's house, Clara was stooping over him, and Lothaire and his mother were standing near. "At last, at last, oh beloved Nathaniel, hast thou recovered from thy serious illness—now thou art again mine!" So spoke Clara, from the very depth of her soul, and clasped Nathaniel in her arms. But with mingled sorrow and delight did the brightly glowing tears fall from his eyes, and he deeply groaned forth: "My own— my own Clara!" Sigismund, who had faithfully remained with his friend in the hour of trouble, now entered. Nathaniel stretched out his hand to him. "And thou, faithful brother, hast not deserted me?" Every trace of Nathaniel's madness had vanished, and he soon gained strength amid the care of his mother, his beloved, and his friends. Good fortune also had visited the house, for an old penurious uncle, of whom nothing had been expected, had died, and had left the mother, besides considerable property, an estate in a pleasant spot near the town.

Thither Nathaniel, with his Clara, whom he now thought of marrying, his mother, and Lothaire, desired to go. Nathaniel had now grown milder and more docile than he had ever been, and he now understood, for the first time, the heavenly purity and the greatness of Clara's mind. No one, by the slightest hint, reminded him of the past. Only, when Sigismund took leave of him, Nathaniel said: "Heavens, brother, I was in an evil way, but a good angel led me betimes to the path of light! Ah, that was Clara!" Sigismund did not let him carry the discourse further for fear that deeply wounding recollections might burst forth bright and flaming. It was about this time that the four happy persons thought of going to the estate. They were crossing, at noon, the streets of the city, where they had made several purchases, and the high steeple of the town-house already cast its gigantic shadow over the market-place. "Oh," said Clara, "let us ascend it once more, and look at the distant mountains!" No sooner said than done. Nathaniel and Clara both ascended the steps, the mother returned home with the servant, and Lothaire, not inclined to clamber up so many steps, chose to remain below. The two lovers stood arm in arm in the highest gallery of the tower, and looked down upon the misty forests, behind which the blue mountains were rising like a gigantic city.

"Look there at that curious little gray bush, which actually seems as if it were striding towards us," said Clara. Nathaniel mechanically put his hand into his breast pocket — he found Coppola's telescope, and he looked on one side. Clara was before the glass. There was a convulsive movement in his pulse and veins, — pale as death, he stared at Clara, but soon streams of fire flashed and glared from his rolling eyes, and he roared frightfully, like a hunted beast. Then he sprang high into the air, and, in the intervals of a horrible laughter, shrieked out, in a piercing tone, "Wooden doll — turn thyself!" Seizing Clara with immense force he wished to hurl her down, but with the energy of a desperate death-struggle she clutched the railings. Lothaire heard the raging of the madman — he heard Clara's shriek of agony — fearful forebodings darted through his mind, he ran up, the door of the second flight was fastened, and the shrieks of Clara became louder and louder. Frantic with rage and anxiety, he dashed against the door, which, at last, burst open. Clara's voice became fainter and fainter. "Help — help — save me!" — with these words the voice seemed to die in the air. "She is gone — murdered by the madman!" cried Lothaire. The door of the gallery was also closed, but despair gave him a giant's strength, and he burst

it from the hinges. Heavens—Clara, grasped by the mad
Nathaniel, was hanging in the air over the gallery,—only
with one hand she still held one of the iron railings. Quick
as lightning Lothaire caught his sister, drew her in, and, at
the same moment, struck the madman in the face with his
clenched fist, so that he reeled and let go his Lothaire ran
down with his fainting sister in his arms. She was saved.
Nathaniel went raging about the gallery and bounded high
in the air, crying, "Fire circle turn thyself—turn thyself!"
The people collected at the sound of the wild shriek, and
among them, prominent by his gigantic stature, was the
advocate Coppelius, who had just come to the town, and
was proceeding straight to the market-place. Some wished
to ascend and secure the madman, but Coppelius laughed,
saying, "Ha, ha,—only wait—he will soon come down of
his own accord," and looked up like the rest. Nathaniel
suddenly stood still as if petrified; he stooped down, perceived Coppelius, and yelling out, "Ah, pretty eyes—pretty
eyes!"—he sprang over the railing.

When Nathaniel lay on the stone pavement, with his
head shattered, Coppelius had disappeared in the crowd.

Many years afterwards it is said that Clara was seen in a
remote spot, sitting hand in hand with a kind-looking man
before the door of a country house, while two lively boys
played before her. From this it may be inferred that she at
last found that quiet domestic happiness which suited her
serene and cheerful mind, and which the morbid Nathaniel
would never have given her.

THE ELEMENTARY SPIRIT

ON the 20th of November, 1815, Albert von B —, lieutenant-colonel in the Prussian service, found himself on the road from Liège to Aix-la-Chapelle. The corps to which he belonged was on its return from France to march to Liège to head-quarters on that very day, and was to remain there for two or three days more. Albert had arrived the evening before; but in the morning he felt himself attacked by a strange restlessness, and — as he would hardly have confessed to himself — an obscure dream, which had haunted him all night, and had foretold that a very pleasant adventure awaited him at Aix-la-Chapelle, was the only cause of his sudden departure. Much surprised even at his own proceeding, he was sitting on the swift horse, which would, he hoped, take him to the city before nightfall.

A severe cutting autumn wind roared over the bare fields, and awakened the voices of the leafless wood in the distance, which united their groans to its howling. Birds of prey came croaking, and followed in flocks the thick clouds which gathered more and more, until the last ray of sunlight had vanished, and a faint dull gray had overspread the entire sky. Albert wrapped his mantle more closely about him, and while he trotted on along the broad road, the picture of the last eventful time unfolded itself to his imagination. He thought how, a few months before, he had travelled on the same road, in an opposite direction, and during the loveliest season of the year. The fields then bloomed forth luxuriantly, the fragrant meadows resembled variegated carpets, and the bushes in which the birds joyously chirped and sung, shone in the fair light of golden sunbeams. The earth, like a longing bride, had richly adorned herself to receive in her dark nuptial chamber the victims consecrated to death — the heroes who fell in the sanguinary battles. Albert had reached the corps to which he was appointed, when the cannon had already begun to thunder by the Sambre, though he was in time enough to take part in the bloody battles of Charleroi, Gilly, and Gosselins. Indeed, chance seemed to wish that Albert should be present just when any thing decided took place.

Thus he was at the last storming of the village Planchenoit, which caused the victory in the most remarkable of all battles — Waterloo. He was in the last engagement of the campaign, when the final effort of rage and fierce despair on the part of the enemy wreaked itself on the immoveable courage of the heroes, who having a fine position in the village of Issy, drove back the foe as they sought, amid the most furious discharge of grape, to scatter death and destruction in the ranks; and indeed drove them back so far, that the sharp-shooters pursued them almost to the barriers of Paris. The night afterwards (that of the 3rd and 4th of July), was, as is well known, that on which the military convention for the surrender of the metropolis was settled at St. Cloud.

The battle of Issy now rose brightly before Albert's soul; he thought of things, which as it seemed, he had not observed, nay, had not been able to observe during the fight. Thus the faces of many individual officers and men appeared before his eyes, depicted in the most lively manner, and his heart was struck by the inexplicable expression, not of proud or unfeeling contempt of death, but of really divine inspiration, which beamed from many an eye. Thus he heard sounds, now exhorting to fight, now uttered with the last sigh of death, which deserved to be treasured up for posterity like the animating utterances of the heroes of antiquity.

"Do I not," thought Albert, "almost feel like one who has a notion of his dream when he wakes, but who does not recollect all its single features till several days afterwards? Ay, a dream, and only a dream, one would think, by flying over time and space, with its mighty wings, could render possible the gigantic, monstrous, unheard-of events, that took place during the eighteen eventful days of a campaign, which mocks the boldest thoughts, the most daring combinations of the speculative mind. Indeed the human mind does not know its own greatness; the act surpasses the thought. For it is not rude physical force, no! it is the mind, which creates deeds as they have happened, and it is the *psychic* power of every single person, really inspired, which attaches itself to the wisdom and genius of the general, and helps to accomplish the monstrous and the unexpected."

Albert was disturbed in these meditations by his groom, who kept about twenty paces behind him, and whom he heard cry out, "Eh! Paul Talkebarth, where the deuce do you come from?" He turned his horse, and perceived that a horseman, who had just trotted past him, and whom he had not particularly observed, was standing still with his groom, beating out the cheeks of the large fox-fur cap with which his head was covered, so that soon the well-known face of Paul Talkebarth, Colonel Victor von S—'s old groom, was made manifest, glowing with the finest vermilion.

Now Albert knew at once what it was that impelled him so irresistibly from Liège to Aix-la-Chapelle, and he could not comprehend how the thought of Victor, his most intimate and dearest friend, whom he had every reason to suppose at Aix, merely lay dimly in his soul, and attained nothing like distinctness. He now also cried out, "Eh! Paul Talkebarth, whence do you come? Where is your master?"

Paul curvetted up to him very gracefully, and said, holding the palm of his hand against the far-too-large cockade of his cap, by way of military salutation: "Yes, 'faith, I am Paul Talkebarth indeed, gracious lieutenant-colonel. We've bad weather here, Zermannöre *(sur mon honneur)*. But the groundsel brings that about. Old Lizzy always used to say so. I cannot say, gracious lieutenant-colonel, if you know Lizzy: she lives at Genthin, but if one has been at Paris, and has seen the wild goat in the Schartinpland *(Jardin des Plantes)*. — Now, what one seeks for one finds near, and here I am in the presence of the gracious lieutenant-colonel, whom I was to seek at Liège. The spirus familis *(spiritus familiaris)* whispered yesterday evening into my master's ear, that the gracious lieutenant-colonel had come to Liège. Zackermannthö *(sacré nom de Dieu)*, there was delight! It may be as it will, but I have never put any faith in the cream-colour. A fine beast, Zermannöre, but a mere childish thing, and the baronness did her utmost — that is true! There are decent sort of people here, but the wine is good for nothing — and when one has been in Paris —! Now, the colonel might have marched in, like one through the Argen trumph *(Arc de triomphe)*, and I should have put the new shabrach on the white horse; gad, how he would have pricked up his ears! But old Lizzy, — she was my aunt, at Genthin, was always accustomed to say — I don't know, gracious lieutenant-colonel, whether you — "

"May your tongue be lamed," said Albert, interrupting the incorrigible babbler. "If your master is at Aix, we must make haste, for we have still above five leagues to go."

"Stop," cried Paul Talkebarth, with all his might; "stop, stop, gracious lieutenant-colonel, the weather is bad here; but for fodder — those who have eyes like us, that shine in the fog."

"Paul," cried Albert, "do not wear out my patience. Where is your master? Is he not in Aix?"

Paul Talkebarth smiled with such delight, that his whole

countenance puckered up into a thousand folds, like a wet glove, and then stretching out his arm he pointed to the building, which might be seen behind the wood, upon a gentle declivity, and said, "Yonder, in the castle!" Without waiting for what Paul might have to prattle further, Albert struck into the path that led from the high road, and hurried on in a rapid trot. After the little that he has said, honest Paul Talkebarth must appear to the gracious reader as an odd sort of fellow. We have only to say, that he being an heir-loom of the family, served Colonel Victor von S— from the moment when the latter first put on his officer's sword, after having been the intendent-general and *maître des plaisirs* of all the sports and mad pranks of his childhood. An old and very odd *magister* who had been tutor to the family through two generations, completed, with the amount of education which he allowed to flow to honest Paul, those happy talents for extraordinary confusion and strange *Eulenspiegelei** with which nature had by no means scantily endued him. At the same time he was the most faithful soul that could possibly exist. Ready every moment to sacrifice his life for his master, neither his advanced age nor any other consideration could prevent the good Paul from following him to the field in the year 1813. His own nature rendered him superior to every hardship; but less strong than his corporeal was his spiritual nature, which seemed to have received a strange shock, or at any rate some extraordinary impulse during his residence in France, especially in Paris. Then, for the first time, did he properly feel that Magister Spreugepileus had been perfectly right when he called him a great light, that would one day shine forth brightly. This shining quality Paul had discovered by the aptness with

---

* *Eulenspiegelei* signifies odd practical jokes, and is derived from Eulenspiegel, the traditional perpetrator of such pleasantries. — J. O.

which he had accommodated himself to the manners of a foreign people, and had learned their language. Therefore, he boasted not a little, and ascribed it to his extraordinary talent alone, that he could often, in respect to quarters and provisions, obtain that which seemed unattainable. Talke-barth's fine French phrases, the gentle reader has already been made acquainted with some pleasant curses — were current, if not through the whole army, at any rate through the corps to which his master was attached. Every trooper who came to quarters in a village, cried to the peasant with Paul's words, "Pisang! de lavendel pur di schevals!" (*Paysan, de l'avoine pour les chevaux.*)

Paul, as is generally the case with eccentric natures, did not like things to happen in the ordinary manner. He was particularly fond of surprises, and sought to prepare them in every possible manner for his master, who was certainly often surprised, though in quite another manner than was designed by honest Talkebarth, whose happy schemes generally failed in their execution. Thus, he now entreated Lieutenant-colonel von B—, when the latter was riding straight up to the principal entrance of the house, to take a circuitous course and enter the court-yard by the back way, that his master might not see him before he entered the room. To meet this view, Albert was obliged to ride over a marshy meadow, where he was grievously splashed by the mud, and then he had to go over a fragile bridge on a ditch. Paul Talkebarth wished to show off his horsemanship by jumping cleverly over; but he fell in with his horse up to the belly, and was with difficulty brought back to firm ground by Albert's groom. Now, in high spirits, he put spurs to his horse, and with a wild huzza leaped into the court-yard. As all the geese, ducks, turkeys, and poultry of the household were gathered together here to rest, while from the one side a flock of sheep, and from the other side a flock of pigs, had been driven in, we may easily imagine that Paul Talkebarth, who not being perfect master of his horse, galloped about the court in large circles, without any will of his own, produced no little devastation in the domestic economy. Amid the fearful noise of squeaking, cackling, bleating, grunting animals, the barking of the dogs, and the scolding of the servants, Albert made his glorious entrance, wishing honest Paul Talkebarth at all the devils, with his project of surprise.

At last Albert leaped from his horse, and entered the house, which, without any claim to beauty or elegance, looked roomy and convenient enough. On the steps he was met by a well-fed, not very tall man, in a short, gray, hunting-jacket, who, with a half-sour smile, said: "Quartered?" By the tone in which the man asked this question, Albert perceived at once that the master of the house, Baron von E— (as he had learned from Paul) was before him. He assured him that he was not quartered, but merely purposed to visit his intimate friend, Colonel Victor von S—, who was, he was told, residing there, and that he only required the baron's hospitality for that evening and the night, as he intended to start very early on the following morning.

The baron's face visibly cleared up, and the full sunshine, which ordinarily seemed to play upon his good-humoured, but somewhat too broad, countenance, returned completely, when Albert as he ascended the stairs with him remarked, that in all probability no division of the army now marching would touch this spot.

The baron opened a door, Albert entered a cheerful-looking parlour, and perceived Victor, who sat with his back towards him. At the sound of his entrance Victor turned round, and with a loud exclamation of joy fell into the arms of the lieutenant. "Is it not true, Albert, you thought of me last night? I knew it, my inner sense told me that you were in Liège at the very moment when you first entered the place. I fixed all my thoughts upon you, my spiritual arms embraced you; you could not escape me."

Albert confessed that—as the gentle reader already knows—dark dreams which came to no clear shape had driven him from Liège.

"Yes," cried Victor, with transport, "yes, it is no fancy, no idle notion; the divine power is given to us, which, ruling space and time, manifests the supersensual in the world of sense."

Albert did not know what Victor meant. Indeed the whole behaviour of his friend, so different from his usual manner, seemed to denote an over-excited state. In the meanwhile the lady, who had been sitting before the fire near Victor, arose and approached the stranger. Albert bowed to her, casting an inquiring glance at Victor. "This is the Baroness Aurora von E—," said Victor, "my hospitable hostess, who tends me ever carefully and faithfully in sickness and in trouble!"

Albert as he looked at the baroness felt quite convinced that the little plump woman had not yet attained her fortieth year, and that she would have been very well made had not the nutritious food of the country, together with much sunshine, caused her shape to deviate a little from the line of beauty. This counteracted the favourable effect of her pretty, fresh-coloured face, the dark blue eyes of which might otherwise have beamed somewhat dangerously for the heart. Albert considered the attire of the baroness almost too homely, for the material of her dress, which was of a dazzling whiteness, while it showed the excellence of the washing and bleaching department, also showed the great distance at which the domestic spinning and weaving stood from perfection. A cotton kerchief, of a very glaring pattern, thrown negligently about the neck, so that its whiteness was visible enough, did not at all increase the brilliant effect of the costume. The oddest thing of all was, that the baroness wore on her little feet the most elegant silken shoes, and on her head the most charming lace cap, after the newest Parisian fashion. This head-dress, it is true, reminded the lieutenant-colonel of a pretty grisette, with whom chance had made him acquainted at Paris, but for this very reason a quantity of uncommonly gallant things flowed from his lips, while he apologised for his sudden appearance. The baroness did not fail to reply to these prettinesses in the proper style, and having once opened her mouth the stream of her discourse flowed on uninterruptedly, till she at last went so far as to say, that it would be impossible to show sufficient attention to such an amiable guest, the friend of the colonel, who was so dear to the family. At the sudden ring of the bell, and the shrill cry: "Mariane, Mariane!" a peevish old woman made her appearance, who, by the bunch of keys which hung from her waist, seemed to be the housekeeper. A consultation was now held with this lady and the husband, as to what nice things could be got ready. It was soon found, however, that all the delicacies, such as venison and the like, were either already consumed, or could only be got the next day. Albert, with difficulty suppressing his displeasure, said, that they would force him to quit immediately in the night, if on his account they disturbed the arrangements of the house in the slightest degree. A little cold meat, nay, some bread and butter, would be sufficient for his supper. The baroness replied by protesting that it was impossible for the lieutenant-colonel to do without something warm, after his ride in the rough, bleak weather, and after a long consultation with Mariane, the preparation of some mulled wine was found to be possible and decided on. Mariane vanished through the doorway, rattling as she went, but at the very moment when they were about to take their seats, the baroness was called out by an amazed maid-servant. Albert overheard that the baroness was being informed at the door of the frightful devastations of Paul Talkebarth, with a list — no inconsiderable one — of the dead, wounded, and missing. The baron ran out after his wife, and while she was scolding he was wishing honest Paul Talkebarth at Jericho, and the servants were uttering general lamentations. Albert briefly told his friend of Paul's exploit in the yard. "That old Eulenspiegel is always playing such tricks," said Victor, angrily, "and yet the rascal means so well from the very bottom of his heart, that one cannot attack him."

At that moment all became quiet without; the chief maid-servant had brought the glad intelligence that Hans Gucklick had been frightened indeed, but had come off free from other harm, and was now eating with a good appetite.

The baron entered with a cheerful mien, and repeated, in a tone of satisfaction, that Hans Gucklick had been spared from that wild, life-disregarding Paul Talkebarth. At the same time he took occasion to expatiate at great length, and from an agricultural point of view, the utility of extending the breeding of poultry. This Hans Gucklick, who had only been very frightened, and had not been otherwise hurt, was the old cock, who was highly prized, and had been for years the pride and ornament of the whole poultry-yard.

The baroness now made her reappearance, but it was only to arm herself with a great bunch of keys, which she took out of a cupboard. Quickly she hurried off, and Albert could hear both her and the housekeeper clattering and rattling up stairs and down stairs, accompanied by the shrill voices of the maid-servants who were called, and the pleasant music of pestles and mortars and graters, which ascended from the kitchen. "Good heavens!" thought Albert. "If the general had marched in with the whole of the head-quarters, there could not have been more noise than has been occasioned by *my* unlucky cup of mulled wine."

The baron, who had wandered from the breeding of poultry to hunting, had not quite got to the end of a very complicated story of a fine deer which he had seen, and had *not* shot, when the baroness entered the room, followed by no less a person than Paul Talkebarth, who bore the mulled wine in a handsome porcelain vessel. "Bring it all here, good Paul," said the baroness, very kindly. Whereupon Paul replied, with an indescribably sweet "A fu zerpir (a *vous servir*), madame." The manes of the victims in the yard seemed to be appeased, and all seemed forgiven.

Now, at last, they all sat down quietly together. The baroness, after she had handed the cup to the visitor, began to knit a monstrous worsted stocking, and the baron took occasion to enlarge upon the species of knitting which was designed to be worn while hunting. During his discourse he seized the vessel, that he also might take a cup. "Ernest!" cried the baroness to him, in an angry tone. He at once desisted from his purpose, and slunk to the cupboard, where he quietly refreshed himself with a glass of Schnapps. Albert availed himself of the moment to put a stop to the baron's tedious disquisitions, by urgently asking his friend how he was going on. Victor was of opinion that there was plenty of time to say, in two words, what had happened to him since their separation, and that he could not expect to hear from Albert's lips all the mighty occurrences of the late portentous period. The baroness assured him, with a smile, that there was nothing prettier than tales of war and murder; while the baron, who had rejoined the party, said that he liked amazingly to bear of battles, when they were very bloody, as they always reminded him of his hunting-parties. He was upon the point of returning to the story of the stag that he did *not* shoot, but Albert cut him short, and laughing out loud, though with increased displeasure, remarked that, though there was, to be sure, some smart shooting in the chase, it was a comfortable arrangement that the stags, hares, etc., whose blood was at stake, could not return the fire.

Albert felt thoroughly warmed by the beverage which he had drunk, and which he found was excellently made of splendid wine, and his comfortable state of body had a good effect on his mind, completely overcoming the ill-humour which had taken possession of him in this uncomfortable society. He unfolded before Victor's eyes the whole sublime and fearful picture of the awful battle, that at once annihilated all the hopes of the fancied ruler of the world. With the most glowing imagination, he described the invincible, lion-like courage of those battalions who at last stormed the village of Planchenoit, and concluded with the words: "Oh! Victor, Victor! would you had been there, and fought with me!"

Victor had moved close to the baroness's chair, and having picked up the large ball of worsted, which had rolled down from her lap, was playing with it in his hands, so that the industrious knitter was compelled to draw the threads through his fingers, and often could not avoid touching his arm with her long needle.

At the words, which Albert uttered with an elevated voice, Victor appeared suddenly to wake as from a dream. He eyed his friend with a singular smile, and said, in a half-suppressed tone: "Yes, dear Albert, what you say is but too true! Man often implicates himself early in snares, the gordian knot of which death alone forcibly sunders! As for what concerns the raising of the devil in general, the audacious invocation of one's own fearful spirit is the most perilous thing possible. But here every thing sleeps!"

Victor's dark, unintelligible words were a sufficient

proof that he had not heard a syllable of all that Albert had said, but had been occupied all the time with dreams, which must have been of a very singular kind.

Albert, as may be supposed, was dumb with amazement. Looking around him he perceived, for the first time, that the master of the house, who with hands folded before him, had sunk against the back of a chair, had dropped his weary head upon his breast, and that the baroness with closed eyes continued to knit mechanically like a piece of clock-work wound up.

Albert sprung up quickly, making a noise as he rose, but at the very same moment the baroness rose also, and approached him with an air, so free, noble, and graceful, that he saw no more of the little, plump, almost comical figure, but thought that the baroness was transformed to another creature. "Pardon the housewife who is employed from break of day, lieutenant-colonel," said she, in a sweet voice, as she grasped Albert's hand, "if in the evening she is unable to resist the effects of fatigue, even though she hears the greatest events recorded in the finest manner. This you must also pardon in the active sportsman. You must certainly be anxious to be alone with your friend and to open your heart to him, and under such circumstances every witness is an incumberance. It will certainly be agreeable to you to take, alone with your friend, the supper which I have served in his apartment."

No proposal could have been more opportune to Albert. He immediately in the most courteous language, wished a good night to his kind hostess, whom he now heartily forgave for the bunch of keys, and the grief about frightened Hans Gucklick, as well as for the stocking-knitting and the nodding.

"Dear Ernest!" cried the baroness, as the friends wished to bid good night to the baron; but as the latter, instead of answering only cried out very plainly: "Huss! Huss! Tyrus! Waldmann! Allons!" and let his head hang on the other side, they tried no more to arouse him from his pleasant dreams.

"Now," said Albert, finding himself alone with Victor for the first time, "tell me how you have fared. But, however, first let us eat a bit, for I am very hungry, and it appears there is something more here than the bread and butter."

The lieutenant-colonel was right, for he found a table elegantly set out with the choicest cold delicacies, the chief ornament of which was a Bayonne ham, and a pasty of red partridges. Paul Talkebarth, when Albert expressed his satisfaction, said, waggishly smiling, that if he had not been present, and had not given Mariane a hint of what it was that the lieutenant-colonel liked, as suppenfink (*super-fine*) — but that, nevertheless, he could not forget his aunt Lizzy, who had burned the rice-pudding on his wedding-day, and that he had now been a widower for thirty years, and one could not tell, since marriages were made in heaven, and that Mariane — but that it was the gracious baroness who had given him the best herself, namely, a whole basket of celery for the gentleman. Albert did not know why such an unreasonable quantity of vegetable food should be served, and was highly delighted, when Paul Talkebarth brought the basket, which contained — not celery — but six bottles of the finest *vin de Sillery*.

While Albert was enjoying himself, Victor narrated how he had come to the estate of the Baron von E—.

The fatigues of the first campaign (1813), which had often proved too much for the strongest constitutions, had ruined Victor's health. The waters at Aix-la-Chapelle would, he hoped, restore him, and he was residing there when Bonaparte's flight from Elba gave the signal for a new and sanguinary contest. When preparations were making for the campaign, Victor received orders from the *Residence* to join the army on the Lower Rhine, if his health permitted; but fate allowed him no more than a ride of four or five leagues. Just before the gate of the house in which the friends now were, Victor's horse, which had usually been the surest and most fearless animal in the world, and had been tried in the wildest tumults of battle, suddenly took fright, and reared, and Victor fell—to use his own words—like a schoolboy who has mounted a horse for the first time. He lay insensible, while the blood flowed from a severe wound in his head, which he had struck against a sharp stone. He was carried into the house, and here, as removal seemed dangerous, he was forced to remain till the time of his recovery, which did not yet seem complete, since, although the wound had been long healed, he was weakened by the attacks of fever. Victor spoke of the care and attention which the baroness had bestowed upon him in terms of the warmest gratitude.

"Well," cried Albert, laughing aloud, "for this I was not prepared. I thought you were going to tell me something very extraordinary, and now, lo, and behold—don't be offended—the whole affair seems to turn out a silly sort of story, like those that have been so worn out in a hundred stupid novels, that nobody with decency can have any thing to do with such adventures. The wounded knight is borne into the castle, the mistress of the house tends him, and he becomes a tender *Amoroso*. For, Victor, that you, in spite of your good taste hitherto, in spite of your whole mode of life, should all of a sudden fall in love with a plump elderly woman, who is homely and domestic to the last degree, that you should play the pining lack-a-daisical youth, who, as somebody says, 'sighs like an oven, and makes songs on his mistress's tears,'—that, I say, I can only look upon as a sort of disease! The only thing that could excuse you in any way, and put you in a poetical light, would be the Spanish Infanta in the 'Physician of his Honour,'* who, meeting a fate similar to yours, fell upon his nose before Donna Menzia's gate, and at last found the beloved one, who unconsciously — "

"Stop!" interrupted Victor, "stop! Don't you think that I see clearly enough, that you take me for a silly dolt? No, no, there is something else — something more mysterious at work. Let us drink!"

The wine, and Albert's lively talk, had produced a wholesome excitement in Victor, who seemed aroused from a gloomy dream. But when, at last, Albert, raising his full glass, said, "Now, Victor, my dear Infanta, here's a health to Donna Menzia, and may she look like our little pet hostess." — Victor cried, laughing, "No, no, I cannot bear that you should take me for a fool. I feel quite cheerful, and ready to make a confession to you of every thing! You must, however, submit to hear an entire youthful period of my life, and it is possible that half the night will be taken up by the narrative."

"Begin!" replied Albert, "for I see we have enough wine to cheer up our somewhat sinking spirits. I only wish it was not so confoundedly cold, nor a crime to wake up the good folks of the house."

"Perhaps," said Victor, "Paul Talkebarth may have made some provision." And, indeed, the said Paul, cursing in his well-known French dialect, courteously assured them, that he had cut small and kept excellent wood for firing, which he was ready to kindle at once. "Fortunately," said Victor, "the same thing cannot happen to me here, that happened at a drysalter's at Meaux, where honest Paul lit me a fire that cost, at least, 1200 francs. The good fellow had got hold of Brazilian sandal-wood, hacked it to pieces, and

---

* Calderón's "Medico de su honra."

put it on the hearth, so that I looked almost like Andolosia, the famous son of the celebrated Fortunatus, whose cook had to light a fire of spices, because the king forbade him to buy wood. You know," continued Victor, as the fire merrily crackled and flamed up, and Paul Talkebarth had left the room, "you know, my dear friend, Albert, that I began my military career in the guards, at Potsdam; indeed, that is nearly all you know of my younger days, because I never had a special opportunity to talk about them — and, still more, because the picture of those years has been represented to my soul in dim outlines, and did not, until I came here, flame up again in bright colours. My first education, in my father's house, does not even deserve the name of a bad one. I had, in fact, no education at all, but was left entirely to my own inclinations, and these indicated any thing rather than a call to the profession of arms. I felt manifestly impelled towards a scientific culture, which the old magister, who was my appointed tutor, and who only liked to be left in quiet, could not give me. At Potsdam I gained with facility a knowledge of modern languages, while I zealously and successfully pursued those studies that are requisite for an officer. I read, besides, with a kind of mania, all that fell into my hands, without selection or regard to utility; however, as my memory was excellent, I had acquired a mass of historical knowledge, I scarcely knew how. People have since done me the honour to assure me that a poetical spirit dwelled in me, which I myself would not rightly appreciate. Certain it is that the *chefs-d'œuvre* of the great poets, of that period, raised me to a state of inspiration of which I had previously no notion. I appeared to myself as another being, developed for the first time into active life. I will only name the 'Sorrows of Werther,' and, more especially, Schiller's 'Robbers.' My fancy received an impulse quite of a different sort from a book, which, for the very reason that it is not finished, gives the mind an impetus that keeps it swinging like a pendulum in constant motion. I mean Schiller's 'Ghostseer.' It may be that the inclination to the mystical and marvellous, which is generally deep-rooted in human nature, was particularly prevalent in me;—whatever was the cause, it is sufficient for me to say that, when I read that book, which seems to contain the exorcising formulæ belonging to the mightiest black art, a magical kingdom, full of super-terrestrial, or, rather, sub-terrestrial marvels, was opened to me, in which I moved about as a dreamer. Once given to this mood, I eagerly swallowed all that would accord with it, and even works of far less worth did not fail in their effect upon me. Thus the 'Genius,' by Grosse, made a deep impression upon me, and I have the less reason to feel ashamed of this, since the first part, at least, on account of the liveliness of the style and the clear treatment of the subject, produced a sensation through the whole literary world. Many an arrest I was obliged to endure, when upon guard, for being absorbed in such a book, or perhaps only in mystic dreams, I did not hear the call, and was forced to be fetched by the inferior officer. Just at this time chance made me acquainted with a very extraordinary man. It happened on a fine summer evening, when the sun had already sunk, and twilight had already begun, that, according to my custom, I was walking alone in a pleasure ground near Potsdam. I fancied that, from the thicket of a little wood, which lay by the road-side, I could hear plaintive sounds, and some words uttered with energy in a language unknown to me. I thought some one wanted assistance, so I hastened to the spot whence the sounds seemed to proceed, and soon, in the red glimmer of the evening, discovered a large, broad-shouldered figure, enveloped in a common military mantle, and stretched upon the ground. Approaching nearer I recognised, to my astonishment, Major O'Malley of the grenadiers. 'Good heavens!' I exclaimed, 'is this you, major? In this situation? Are you ill? Can I help you?' The major looked at me with a fixed, wild stare, and then said, in a harsh voice, 'What the devil brings you here, lieutenant? What does it matter to you whether I lie here or not? Go back to the town!' Nevertheless, the deadly paleness of O'Malley's face made me suspect that there was something wrong, and I declared that I would not leave him, but would only return to the town in his company. 'Good!' said the major, quite coldly and deliberately, after he had remained silent for some moments, and had endeavoured to raise himself, in which attempt, as it appeared to be attended with difficulty, I assisted him. I perceived now that—as was frequently the case when he went out in the evening—he had nothing but a shirt under the cloak, which was a common *commis-mantel* as they call it, that he had put on his boots, and that he wore upon his bald head his officer's hat, with broad gold lace. A pistol, which lay on the ground near him, he caught up hastily, and, to conceal it from me, put it into the pocket of his cloak. During the whole way to the town he did not speak a syllable to me, but now and then uttered disjointed phrases in his own language—he was an Irishman by birth—which I did not understand. When he had reached his quarters he pressed my hand, and said, in a tone in which there was something indescribable—something that had never been heard before, and which still echoes in my soul: 'Good night, lieutenant! Heaven guard you, and give you good dreams!' This Major O'Malley was one of the strangest men possible, and if, perhaps, I except a few somewhat eccentric Englishmen, whom I have met, I know no officer in the whole great army to compare in outward appearance with O'Malley. If it be true—as some travellers affirm—that nature nowhere produces such peculiarities as in Ireland, and that, therefore, every family can exhibit the prettiest cabinet pictures, Major O'Malley would justly serve as a prototype for all his nation. Imagine a man strong as a tree, six feet high, whose build could scarcely be called awkward, but none of whose limbs fitted the rest, so that his whole figure seemed huddled together, as in that game where figures are composed of single parts, the numbers on which are decided by the throw of the dice. An aquiline nose, and delicately formed lips would have given a noble appearance to his countenance, but his prominent glassy eyes were almost repulsive, and his black bushy eyebrows had the character of a comic mask. Strangely enough there was something lachrymose in the major's face whenever he laughed, which, by the way, seldom happened, while he seemed to laugh whenever the wildest passion mastered him, and in this laugh there was something so terrific, that the oldest and most stout-hearted fellows would shudder at it. But, however, seldom as Major O'Malley laughed, it was just as seldom that he allowed himself to be carried away by passion. That the major should ever have an uniform to fit him seemed an utter impossibility. The best tailors in the regiment failed utterly when they applied their art to the formless figure of the major; his coat, though cut according to the most accurate measure, fell into unseemly folds, and hung on his body as if placed there to be brushed, while his sword dangled against his legs, and his hat sat upon his head in such a queer fashion that the military schismatic might be recognised a hundred paces off. A thing quite unheard of in those days in which there was so much pedantry in matters of form — O'Malley wore no tail! To be sure a tail could scarcely have been fastened to the few gray locks that curled at the back of his head, and, with the exception of these, he was perfectly bald. When the major rode, people expected every moment to see him tumble from his horse, when he fought they expected to see him beaten; and yet he was the very best rider and fencer, — in a word, the very best *Gymnastiker* that could exist.

"This will suffice to give you the picture of a man, whose whole mode of life might be called mysterious, as he now threw away large sums, now seemed in want of assistance, and removed from all the control of superiors, and every restraint of service, could do exactly as he liked. And even that which he did like was so eccentric, or rather so splenetically mad, that one felt uneasy about his sanity. They said that the major, at a certain period, when Potsdam and its environs was the scene of a strange mystification, that even found a place in the history of the day, had played an important part, and still stood in certain relations, which caused the incomprehensibility of his position. A book of very ill-repute, which appeared at the time — it was called 'Excorporations,' if I mistake not, — and which contained the portrait of a man very like the major, increased that belief, and I, struck by the mysterious contents of this book, felt the more inclined to consider O'Malley a sort of Arminian, the more I observed his chimerical, I may almost say supernatural proceedings. He himself gave me additional opportunity to make such observations, for since the evening on which I found him ill, or otherwise overcome, in the wood, he had taken an especial fancy to me, so that it seemed absolutely necessary for him to see me every day. To describe to you the whole peculiarity of this intercourse with the major, to tell you a great deal that seemed to confirm the judgment of the men, who boldly maintained that he had second-sight, and was in compact with the devil, would be superfluous, as you will soon have sufficient knowledge of the awful spirit that was destined to disturb the peace of my life.

"I was on guard at the castle, and there received a visit from my cousin, Captain von T—, who had come with a young officer from Berlin to Potsdam. We were indulging in friendly converse over our wine, when, towards midnight, Major O'Malley entered. 'I thought to find you alone, lieutenant,' said he, casting glances of displeasure at my guests, and he wished to depart at once. The captain then reminded him that they were old acquaintance, and at my request he consented to remain.

"'Your wine,' exclaimed O'Malley, as he tossed down a bumper, after his usual manner; 'your wine, lieutenant, is the vilest stuff that ever tortured an honest fellow's bowels. Let us see if this is of a better sort.'

"He then took a bottle from the pocket of the cloak which he had drawn over his shirt, and filled the glasses. We pronounced the wine excellent, and considered it to be very fiery Hungarian.

"Somehow or other, I cannot say how, conversation turned upon magical operations, and particularly upon the book of ill report, to which I have already alluded. The captain, especially when he had drunk wine, had a certain scoffing tone, which every one could not endure, and in this tone he began to talk about military exorcisors and wizards, who had done very pretty things at that time, so that even at the present time people revered their power, and made offerings to it. 'Whom do you mean?' cried O'Malley, in a threatening tone; 'whom do you mean, captain? If you mean me, we will put the subject of raising spirits aside; I can show you that I understand the art of conjuring the soul out of the body, and for that art I require no talisman but my sword or a good pistol-barrel.'

"There was nothing the captain desired less than a quarrel with O'Malley. He therefore gave a neat turn to the subject, asserting that he did indeed mean the major, but intended nothing but a jest, which was, perhaps, an ill-timed one. Now, however, he would ask the major in earnest,

whether he would not do well by contradicting the silly ru-
mour, that he commanded mysterious powers, and thus,
in his own person, check the foolish superstition, which by
no means accorded with an age so enlightened. The major
leaned completely across the table, rested his head on both
his fists, so that his nose was scarcely a span removed from
the captain's face, and then said very calmly, staring at him
with his prominent eyes: 'Even, friend, if Heaven has not
blessed you with a very penetrating intellect, I hope you
will be able to see, that it is the silliest conceit, nay, I may
say, the most atrocious presumption to believe that with our
own spiritual existence every thing is concluded, and that
there are no spiritual beings, which, differently endowed
from ourselves, often from their own nature alone, make
themselves temporary forms, manifest themselves in space
and time, and further, aiming at a sort of reaction, can take
refuge in the mass of clay, which we call a body. I do not
reproach you, captain, for not having read, and for being
ignorant of every thing that cannot be learned at a review
or on parade, but this I will tell you, that if you had peeped
now and then into clever books, and knew Cardanus, Jus-
tin Martyr, Lactantius, Cyprian, Clement of Alexandria,
Macrobius, Trismegistus, Nollius, Dorneus, Theophrastus,
Fludd, William Postel, Mirandola; nay, even the cabalistic
Jews, Josephus and Philo, you might have had an inkling
of things which are at present above your horizon, and of
which you therefore have no right to talk.'

"With these words O'Malley sprang up, and walked
up and down with heavy steps, so that the windows and
glasses vibrated.

"The captain, somewhat astonished, assured the major, that although he had the highest esteem for his learn-
ing, and did not wish to deny that there were, nay, must
be, higher spiritual natures, he was firmly convinced that

any communication with an unknown spiritual world was contrary to the very conditions of humanity, and therefore impossible, and that any thing advanced as a proof of the contrary, was based on self-delusion or imposture.

"After the captain had been silent for a few seconds, O'Malley suddenly stood still, and began, 'Captain, or,' — turning to me, — 'lieutenant, do me the favour to sit down and write an epic as noble and as superhumanly great as the Iliad.'

"We both answered, that neither of us would succeed, as neither of us had the Homeric genius. 'Ha! ha!' cried the major, 'mark that, captain! Because your mind is incapable of conceiving and bringing forth the divine; nay, because your nature is not so constituted, that it can even kindle into the knowledge of it, you presume to deny that such things are possible with any one. I tell you, the intercourse with higher spiritual natures depends on a particular *psychic* organisation. That organisation, like the creative power of poetry, is a gift which the spirit of the universe bestows upon its favourites.'

"I read in the captain's face, that he was on the point of making some satirical reply to the major. To stop this, I took up the conversation myself; and remarked to the major that, as far as I had any knowledge of the subject, the cabalists prescribed certain rules and forms, that intercourse with unknown spiritual beings might be attained. Before the major could reply, the captain, who was heated with wine, sprang from his seat, and said bitterly, 'What is the use of all this talking? You give yourself out as a superior being, major, and want to believe, that because you are made of better stuff than any of us, you command spirits! You must allow me to believe that you are nothing but a besotted dreamer, until you give us some ocular demonstration of your *psychic* power.'

"The major laughed wildly, and said, 'So, captain, you take me for a common necromancer, a miserable juggler, do you? That accords with your limited view! However, you shall be permitted to take a peep into a dark region of which you have no notion, and which may, perhaps, have a destructive effect upon you. I warn you against it, and would have you reflect, that your mind may not be strong enough to bear many things, which to me would be no more than agreeable pastime.'

"The captain protested that he was quite ready to cope with all the spirits and devils that O'Malley could raise, and we were obliged to give our word of honour to the major that we would meet him at ten o'clock on the night of the autumnal equinox, at the inn near the — gate, when we should learn more.

"In the meanwhile it had become clear daylight; the sun was shining through the window. The major then placed himself in the middle of the room, and cried with a voice of thunder, 'Incubus! Incubus! Nehmahmihah Scedim!' He then threw off his cloak, which he had not yet laid aside, and stood in full uniform.

"At that moment I was obliged to leave the room as the guard was getting under arms. When I returned, the major and the captain had both vanished.

"'I only stayed behind,' said the young officer, a good, amiable youth, whom I found alone. — 'I only stayed behind to warn you against this major, this fearful man! I will have nothing to do with his fearful secrets, and I only regret that I have given my word to be present at a deed, which will be destructive, perhaps, to us all, and certainly to the captain. You may depend upon it that I am not inclined to believe in the tales that old nurses tell to children; but did you observe that the major successively took eight bottles from his pocket, that seemed scarcely large enough to hold one? — that at last, although he wore nothing but his shirt under his cloak, he suddenly stood attired by invisible hands?' It was, indeed, as the lieutenant had said, and I felt an icy shudder come over me.

"On the appointed day the captain called upon me with my young friend, and at the stroke of ten we were at the inn as we had promised the major. The lieutenant was silent and reserved, but the captain was so much the louder and in high spirits. 'Indeed!' he cried, when it was already half-past ten, and no O'Malley had made his appearance, 'indeed I believe that the conjuror has left us in the lurch with all his spirits and devils!' — 'That he has not,' said a voice close behind the captain, and O'Malley was among us without any one having seen how he entered. The laugh, into which the captain was about to break, died away.

"The major, who was dressed as usual in his military cloak, thought that there was time to drink a few glasses of punch before he took us to the place where he designed to fulfill his promise. It would do us good as the night was cold and rough, and we had a tolerably long way to go. We sat down at a table, on which the major had laid some links bound together, and a book.

"'Ho ho!' cried the captain, 'this is your conjuring book, is it, major?'

"'Most assuredly,' replied O'Malley, drily. "The captain seized the book, opened it, and at that moment laughed so immoderately, that we did not know what could have struck him, as being so very ridiculous.

"'Come,' said he, recovering himself with difficulty,' come, this is too bad! What the devil, major — oh, you want to play your tricks upon us, or have you made some mistake? Only look here, comrades!'

"You may conceive our astonishment, friend Albert, when we saw that the book which the captain held before our eyes, was no other than 'Peplier's French Grammar.' O'Malley took the book out of the captain's hand, put it into the pocket in his cloak, and then said very quietly — indeed his whole demeanour was quiet and milder than usual — 'It must be very immaterial to you, captain, of what instruments I make use to fulfill my promise, which only binds me to give you a sensible demonstration of my intercourse with the world of spirits which surrounds us, and which, in fact, comprises the condition of our higher being. Do you think that my power requires such paltry crutches as especial mystical forms, choice of a particular time, a remote awful spot — things which paltry cabalists are in the habit of employing for their useless experiments? In the open market-place, at every hour, I could show you my power; and when, after you had presumptuously enough challenged me to enter the lists, I chose a particular time, and, as you will perceive, a place that you may think rather awful, I only wished to show a civility to him, who, on this occasion, is to be in some sort your guest. One likes to receive guests in one's best room, and at the most suitable hour.'

"It struck eleven, the major took up the torches, and desired us to follow him.

"He strode so quickly along the high road that we had a difficulty in following him, and when we had reached the toll-house, turned into a footpath on the right, that led to a thick wood of firs. After we had run for nearly an hour, the major stood still, and told us to keep close behind him, as we might otherwise lose ourselves in the thicket of the wood that we now had to enter. We went through the densest bushes, so that one or the other of us was constantly caught by the uniform or the sword, so as to extricate himself with difficulty, until at last we came to an open space. The moonbeams were breaking through the dark clouds, and I perceived the ruins of a large building, into which the major strode. It grew darker and darker; the major desired us to stand still, as he wished to conduct every one of us down singly. He began with the captain, and my turn came next. The major clasped me round, and I was more carried by him than I walked into the depth. 'Stop here,' whispered the major, 'stop here quietly till I have fetched the lieutenant, then my work shall begin.'

"Amid the impenetrable darkness I heard the breathing of a person who stood close by me. 'Is that you, captain?' I exclaimed. 'Certainly it is,' replied the captain, 'have a care, cousin; this will all end in foolish jugglery, but it is a cursed place to which the major has brought us, and I wish we were sitting at a bowl of punch, for my limbs are all trembling with cold, and, if you will have it so, with a certain childish apprehension.'

"It was no better with me than with the captain. The boisterous autumn wind whistled and howled through the walls, and a strange groaning and whispering answered it from below. Scared night birds swept fluttering by us, while a low whining noise seemed to be gliding away close to the ground. Truly both the captain and myself might say of the horrors of our situation the same thing that Cervantes says of Don Quixote, when he passes the portentous night before the adventure with the fulling-mills: 'One less courageous would have lost his presence of mind altogether.' The splashing of some water in the vicinity, and the barking of dogs, showed that we were not far from the leather-manufactory, which is by the river in the neighbourhood of Potsdam. We at last heard some dully sounding steps, which became nearer and nearer until the major cried out close to us: 'Now we are together, and that which we have begun can be completed.' By means of a chemical fire-box he kindled the torches which he had brought with him and stuck them in the ground. They were seven in number. We found that we were in the ruined vault of a cellar. O'Malley ranged us in a half-circle, threw off his cloak and shirt, so that he remained naked to the waist, and opening the book began to read as follows, in a voice that more resembled the dull roaring of a distant beast of prey than the sound of a human being: 'Monsieur, pretez moi un peu, s'il vous plaît, votre canif. — Oui, Monsieur, d'abord — le voilà, je vous le rendrai.'"

"Come," said Albert, here interrupting his friend, "this is indeed too bad! The dialogue 'On writing,' from Peplier's Grammar, as a formula for exorcism! And you did not laugh out and bring the whole thing to an end at once?"

"I am now," continued Victor, "coming to a moment which I doubt whether I shall succeed in describing. May your fancy only give animation to my words! The major's voice grew more awful, while the wind howled more loudly, and the flickering light of the torches covered the walls with strange forms, that changed as they flitted by. I felt the cold perspiration dripping on my forehead, and forcibly succeeded in preserving my presence of mind, when a cutting tone whistled through the vault, and close before my eyes stood something — "

"How?" cried Albert. "Something! What do you mean, Victor? A frightful form?"

"It sounds absurd," continued Victor, "to talk of 'a formless form,' but I can find no other word to express the hideous something that I saw. It is enough to say that at that moment the horror of hell thrust its pointed ice-dagger into my heart, and I became insensible. At broad mid-day I found myself undressed and lying upon my couch. All the horrors of the night had passed, and I felt quite well and easy. My young friend, the lieutenant, was asleep in the arm-chair. As soon as I stirred he awoke, and testified the greatest joy at finding me in perfect health. From him I learned that as soon as the major had begun his gloomy work, he had closed his eyes, and had endeavoured closely to follow the dialogue from Peplier's Grammar, without regarding any thing else. Notwithstanding all his efforts, a fearful apprehension, hitherto unknown, had gained the mastery over him, though he preserved his consciousness. The frightful whistle, was, he said, followed by wild laughter. He had once involuntarily opened his eyes, and perceived the major, who had again thrown his mantle round him, and was upon the point of taking upon his shoulders the captain, who lay senseless on the ground. 'Take care of your friend,' cried O'Malley to the lieutenant, and giving him a torch, he went up with the captain. The lieutenant then spoke to me, as I stood there immoveable, but it was to no purpose. I seemed quite paralysed, and he had the greatest difficulty in bringing me into the open air. Suddenly the major returned, took me on his shoulders, and carried me away as he had carried the captain before. But what was the horror of the lieutenant, when on leaving the wood, he saw a second O'Malley who was carrying the captain along the broad path! However, silently praying to himself, he got the better of his horror, and followed me, firmly resolved not to quit me, happen what might, till we reached my quarters, where O'Malley set me down and left me, without speaking a word. With the help of my servant,—who even then was my honest Eulenspiegel, Paul Talkebarth; the lieutenant had brought me into my room, and put me to bed.

"Having concluded this narrative, my young friend implored me, in the most touching manner, to shun all association with the terrible O'Malley. The physician, who had been called in, found the captain in the inn by the gate, where we had assembled, struck speechless by apoplexy. He recovered, indeed, but remained unfit for the service, and was forced to quit it. The major had vanished, having, as the officers said, obtained leave of absence. I was glad that I did not see him again, for a deep indignation had mingled itself with the horror which his dark mode of life occasioned. My cousin's misfortune was the work of O'Malley, and it seemed my duty to take a sanguinary revenge. ...

"A considerable time had elapsed, and the remembrance of that fatal night grew faint. The occupations required by the service overcame my propensity to mystical dreaming. A book then fell into my hands, the effect of which, on my whole being, seemed perfectly inexplicable, even to myself. I mean that strange story of Cazotte's, which is known in a German translation as 'Teufel Amor' (The Devil Love). My natural bashfulness, nay, a kind of childish timidity, had kept me from the society of ladies, while the particular direction of my mind resisted every ebullition of rude passion. Now, for the first time, was a sensual tendency revealed in me which I had never suspected. My pulse beat high, a consuming fire coursed through nerves and veins, as I went through those scenes of the most dangerous, nay, most horrible love, which the poet had described in the most glowing colours. I saw, I heard, I was sensible to nothing but the charming Biondetta. I sank under the pleasing torments, like Alvarez —"

"Stop, stop!" interrupted Albert, "I have no very clear remembrance of Cazotte's 'Diable Amoureux;' but, so far as I recollect, the whole story turns upon the circumstance that a young officer of the guards, in the service of the King of Naples, is tempted by a mystical comrade to raise the devil in the ruins of Portici. When he has uttered the formula of exorcism, a hideous camel's head, with a long neck, thrust itself towards him out of a window, and cries, in a horrible voice, 'Che vuoi.' Alvarez — so is the young officer named — commands the spectre to appear in the shape of a spaniel, and then in that of a page. This happens; but the page soon becomes a most charming, amorous girl, and completely entangles the enchanter. How Cazotte's pretty story concludes has quite escaped me."

"That is at present quite immaterial," said Victor; "but you will perhaps be reminded of it by the conclusion to my story. Attribute it to my propensity to the wonderful, and also to something mysterious which I experienced, that Cazotte's tale soon appeared to me a magic mirror, in which I could discern my own fate. Was not O'Malley to me that mystical Dutchman who decoyed Alvarez by his arts?

"The desire which glowed in my heart, of achieving the terrible adventure of Alvarez, filled me with horror; but even this horror made me tremble with unspeakable delight, such as I had never before known. Often did a wish arise within me, that O'Malley would return and place in my arms the hell-birth, to which my entire self was abandoned, and I could not kill the sinful hope and deep abhorrence which again darted through my heart like a dagger. The strange mood produced by my excited condition remained a mystery to all; they thought I suffered from some morbid state of mind, and sought to cheer me and dissipate my gloomy thoughts. Under the pretext of some service, they sent me to the *Residence,* where the most brilliant circle was open to me. But if I had always been shy and bashful, society — especially the approach of ladies — now produced in me absolute repugnance. The most charming only seemed to scoff at Biondetta's image which I bore within me. When I returned to Potsdam, I shunned all association with my comrades, and my favourite abode was the wood — the scene of those frightful events that had nearly cost my poor cousin his life. I stood close by the ruins, and, being impelled by an undefined desire, was on the point of making my way in, through the thick brushwood, when I suddenly saw O'Malley, who walked slowly out, and did not seem to perceive me. My long repressed anger boiled up instantly, I darted upon the major, and told him in few words, that he must fight with me on account of my cousin. 'Be it so at once,' said the major, coldly and gravely, and he threw off his mantle, drew his sword, and at the very first pass struck mine out of my hand with irresistible force and dexterity. 'We will fight with pistols,' cried I, wild with rage, and was about to pick up my sword, when O'Malley held me fast, and said, in a calm mild tone, such as I had scarcely ever heard from him before: 'Do not be a fool, my son! You see that I am your superior in fighting; you could sooner wound the air than me, and I could never prevail on myself to stand in a hostile position to you, to whom I owe my life, and indeed something more.' The major then took me by the arm, and gently drawing me along, proved to me that the captain alone had been the cause of his own misfortune, since, in spite of every warning, he had ventured on things to which he was unequal, and had forced the major to do what he did, by his ill-timed and insulting raillery. I myself cannot tell what a singular magic there was in O'Malley's words, nay, in his whole manner. He not only succeeded in quieting me, but had such an effect upon me, that I involuntarily revealed to him the secret of my internal condition — of the destructive warfare that was carried on within my soul. 'The particular constellation,' said O'Malley, when I had finished, 'which rules over you, my son, has now ordained that a silly book should make you attentive to your own internal being. I call the book silly, because it treats of a goblin that is at once repulsive and without character. What you ascribe to the effect of these licentious images of the poet, is nothing but an impulse towards an union with a spiritual being of another region, which results from your happily constituted organisation. If you had shown more confidence in me, you would have been on a higher grade

long ago. However, I will take you as my scholar.' O'Malley
now began to make me acquainted with the nature of elementary spirits. I understood little that he said, but all referred to the doctrine of sylphs, undines, salamanders, and
gnomes, such as you may find in the dialogues of the Comte
de Cabalis. He concluded by prescribing me a particular
course of life, and thought that in the course of a year I
might obtain my Biondetta, who would certainly not do me
the wrong of changing into the incarnate Satan in my arms.
With the same ardour as Alvarez, I thought that I should
die of impatience in so long a time, and would venture any
thing to attain my end sooner. The major remained reflect-
ing in silence for some moments, and then said: 'It is certain
that an elementary spirit is seeking your good graces. This
may enable you to obtain that in a short time, for which others strive during whole years. I will cast your horoscope.
Perhaps your mistress will reveal herself to me. In nine
days you shall hear more.' I actually counted the hours,
feeling now penetrated by a mysterious delightful hope,
and now as if I had involved myself in a dangerous affair.
Late in the evening of the ninth day, the major at last entered my room, and desired me to follow him. 'Are we to go
to the ruins?' I asked. 'Certainly not,' replied O'Malley,
smiling, 'for the work which we now have in hand, we want
neither a remote awful spot, nor a terrible exorcism out of
Peplier's grammar. Besides, my incubus can have no part in
today's experiment, which, properly speaking, you under-
take, not I.' The major conducted me to his quarters, and
there explained to me that the matter was to procure something by means of which my own *self* might be opened to
the elementary spirit, and the latter might have the power
of revealing itself to me in the invisible world, and holding
intercourse with me. This *something* was what the Jewish
cabalists called 'Teraphim.' He now pushed aside a book-

case, opened the door concealed behind it, and we entered a little vaulted cabinet, in which, besides all sorts of strange unknown utensils, I saw a complete apparatus for chemical — or, as I might almost believe — alchemical experiments. From the flaring charcoal on a small hearth were darting forth little blue flames. Before this hearth I had to sit opposite the major, and to uncover my bosom. I had no sooner done this, than the major, before I was aware of it, scratched me with a lancet under the left breast, and caught in a little vial the few drops of blood that flowed from the slight wound, which I could scarcely feel. He next took a bright plate of metal, polished like a mirror, poured upon it first another vial that contained a reddish liquid, and afterwards the one filled with my blood, and then held the plate close over the charcoal fire. I was seized with deep horror, when I thought I saw a long, pointed, glaring tongue rise serpent-like upon the coals, and greedily lick away the blood from the metallic mirror. The major now told me to look into the fire with a mind firmly fixed. I did so, and soon I seemed to behold, as in a dream, a number of confused forms, flashing through one another on the metal, which the major still held over the charcoal. Suddenly, I felt in my breast, where the major had scratched my skin, such a strong, piercing pain, that I involuntarily shrieked aloud. 'Won! Won!' cried O'Malley at that instant, and, rising from his seat, he placed before me on the hearth a little doll, about two inches long, into which the metal seemed to have formed itself. 'That,' said the major, 'is your Teraphim. The favours of the elementary spirit towards you seem to be more than ordinary. You may now venture on the utmost.' At the major's bidding, I took the little figure, from which, though it looked red-hot, only a genial warmth was streaming, pressed it to the wound, and placed myself before a round mirror, from which the major had withdrawn the covering. 'Force your wishes,' said O'Malley, 'to the greatest intensity, which will not be difficult, as the Teraphim is operating, and utter in the sweetest tone of which you are capable, the word —.' To tell you the truth, I have forgotten the strange-sounding word, which was spoken by O'Malley. Scarcely had half the syllables passed my lips, than an ugly, madly-distorted face grinned at me spitefully from the mirror. 'In the name of all the devils, whence come you, you accursed dog?' yelled O'Malley behind me. I turned round, and saw my Paul Talkebarth, who was standing in the door-way, and whose handsome face was reflected in the magic mirror. The major, wild with rage, flew at honest Paul; yet, before I could get between them, O'Malley stood close to him, perfectly motionless, and Paul availed himself of the opportunity to make a prolix apology; saying, how he had looked for me, how he had found the door open, how he had walked in, etc. 'Begone, rascal,' said O'Malley at last, in a quieter tone, and when I added, 'Go, good Paul, I will return home directly,' the Eulenspiegel departed quite terrified and confounded. "I had held the doll fast in my hand, and O'Malley assured me, that it was owing to this circumstance alone, that all our labour had not been in vain. Talkebarth's ill-timed intrusion had, however, delayed the completion of the work for a long time. He advised me to turn off that faithful servant, but this I had not the heart to do. Moreover, he assured me that the elementary spirit which had shown me such favour, was nothing less than a salamander, as indeed, he suspected, when he cast my horoscope and found that Mars stood in the first house. I now come again to moments of which you can have but a slight notion, as words are incapable of describing them. The Devil Amor, Biondetta — all was forgotten; I thought only of my Teraphim. For whole hours I could look at the doll, as it lay on the table before me, and the glow of love that streamed through my veins seemed then, like the heavenly fire of Prometheus, to animate the little figure which grew up as in ardent longing. But this form vanished as soon as I had thought it, and the unspeakable anguish which cut through my heart, was associated with a strange indignation, that impelled me to fling the doll away from me as a miserable ridiculous toy. Yet when I grasped it, an electric shock seemed to dart through all my limbs, and I felt as if a separation from the talisman of love would annihilate me. I will openly confess to you that my passion, although the proper object of it was an elementary spirit, was directed among all sorts of equivocal dreams towards objects in the miserable world that surrounded me, so that my excited fancy made now this, now that lady, the representative of the coy salamander that eluded my embrace. I confessed my wrong, indeed, and entreated my little mystery to pardon my infidelity; but by the declining power of that strange crisis, which had ordinarily moved my inmost soul with glowing love, nay, by a certain unpleasant void, I could plainly feel that I was receding from my object rather than approaching it. And yet the passions of a youth, blooming in full vigour, seemed to deride my mystery and my repugnance. I trembled at the slightest touch of a charming woman, though I found myself red with blushes. Chance conducted me again to the *Residence.* I saw the Countess von L —, the most charming woman, and the greatest lover of conquests that then shone in the first circles of Berlin. She cast her glances upon me, and the mood in which I then was, naturally rendered it very easy for her to lure me completely into her toils. Nay, she at last induced me to reveal my whole soul, without reserve, to discover my secret, and even to show her the mysterious image that I wore upon my breast."

"And," interrupted Albert, "did she not laugh at you heartily, and call you a besotted youth?"

"Nothing of the sort," continued Victor; "she listened to me with a seriousness which she had not shown on any other occasion, and when I had finished, she implored me, with tears in her eyes, to renounce the diabolical arts of the infamous O'Malley. Taking me by both my hands, and looking at me with an expression of the tenderest love, she spoke of the dark practices of the cabalistic art in a manner so learned and so profound, that I was not a little surprised. But my astonishment reached the highest point, when she called the major the most abandoned, abominable traitor, for trying to lure me into destruction by his black art, when I had saved his life. Weary of existence, and in danger of being crushed to the earth by the deepest ignominy, O'Malley was, it seems, on the point of shooting himself, when I stepped in and prevented the suicide, for which he no longer felt any inclination, as the evil that oppressed him had been averted. The countess concluded by assuring me, that if the major had plunged me into a state of psychic distemper, she would save me, and that the first step to that end would consist in my delivering the little image into her hands. This I did readily, for thus I thought I should, in the most beautiful manner, be freed from a useless torment. The countess would not have been what she really was had she not let a lover pine a long time in vain,—and this course she pursued with me. At last, however, my passion was to be requited. At midnight a confidential servant waited for me at the back door of the palace, and led me through distant passages into an apartment which the god of love seemed to have decorated. There I was to expect the countess. Half overcome by the fumes of the fine scents that wound through the chamber, trembling with love and expectation, I stood in the midst of the room. All at once a glance darted through my soul like a flash of lightning—"

"How!" cried Albert, "a glance, and no eyes! And you saw nothing? Another formless form!"

"You may find it incomprehensible," said Victor, "but so it was; I could see no form — nothing, and yet I felt the glance deep in my bosom, and a sudden pain quivered at the spot which O'Malley had wounded. At the same moment I perceived upon the chimney-piece my little image, grasped it, darted from the room, commanded the terrified servant, with a threatening gesture, to lead me down, ran home, awakened my man Paul, and had all my things packed up. At the earliest hour of morning I was already on my way back to Potsdam. I had passed several months at the *Residence,* my comrades were delighted at my unexpected return, and kept me fast the whole day, so that I did not return to my quarters till late at night. I placed the darling image I had recovered upon the table, and, no longer able to resist the effects of fatigue, threw myself on my couch without undressing. Soon a dreamy feeling came over me, as if I were surrounded by a beaming light; — I awoke; — I opened my eyes, and the room was indeed gleaming with magical radiance. But — Oh, Heavens! — on the same table on which I had laid the doll, I perceived a female figure, who, resting her head on her hand, appeared to slumber. I can only tell you that I never dreamed of a more delicate or graceful form — a more lovely face. To give you a notion in words of the strange mysterious magic, which beamed from this lovely figure, I am not able. She wore a silken flame-coloured dress, which, fitting tight to the waist and bosom, reached only to the ankles, exhibiting her delicately formed feet; the lovely arms, which were bare to the shoulders, and seemed both from their colour and form to have been breathed by Titian, were adorned with bracelets; in her brown, somewhat reddish hair, a diamond sparkled."

"Oh!" said Albert, smiling, "thy salamandrine has no very exquisite taste. With reddish brown hair, she dresses in flame-coloured silk."

"Do not jest," continued Victor, "do not jest. I repeat to you that under the influence of a mysterious magic, my breath was stopped. At last a deep sigh escaped my oppressed bosom. She then opened her eyes, raised herself, approached me, and grasped my hand. All the glow of the most ardent love darted like a flash of lightning through my soul, when she gently pressed my hand, and whispered with the sweetest voice, — ' Yes, thou hast conquered — thou art my ruler — I am thine!' — 'Oh, thou child of the Gods — thou heavenly being!' I cried aloud; and embracing her, I pressed her close to my bosom. But at that instant the creature melted away in my arms."

"How!" said Albert, interrupting his friend, "in Heaven's name, melted away?"

"Melted away," continued Victor, "in my arms. In no other manner can I describe to you my sensation of the incomprehensible disappearance of that lovely being. At the same time the glittering light was extinguished, and I fell, I do not know how, into a profound sleep. When I awoke I held the doll in my hand. I should weary you if I were to tell you more of my strange intercourse with that mysterious being, which now began and lasted for several weeks, than by saying that the visit was repeated every night in the same manner. Much as I strove against it, I could not resist the dreamy situation which came over me, and from which the lovely being awoke me with a kiss. She remained with me longer and longer on every occasion. She said much concerning mysterious things, but I listened more to the sweet melody of her voice, than to the words themselves. Even by day-time I often seemed to feel the warm breath of some being near me; nay, I often heard a whispering, a sighing close by me in society, especially when I spoke with any lady, so that all my thoughts were directed to my lovely mysterious mistress, and I was dumb and lifeless for all surrounding objects. It once happened at a party that a lady bashfully approached me to give me the kiss which I had won at a game of forfeits. But when I bent to her I felt — before my lips had touched hers — a loud kiss upon my mouth, and a soft voice whispered at the same time, 'To me alone do your kisses belong.' Both I and the lady were somewhat alarmed, while the rest of the party thought we had kissed in reality. This kiss I held to be a sign that Aurora — so I called my mysterious mistress — would now for good and all take some living shape, and no more leave me. When the lovely one again appeared to me on the following night, I entreated her in the usual manner, and in the most touching words, such as the ardour of love inspired to complete my happiness, and to be mine for ever in a visible form. She gently extricated herself from my arms, and then said with mild earnestness, 'You know in what manner you became my master. My happiest wish was to belong to you entirely; but the fetters that bind me to the throne to which the race, of which I am one, is subjected, are only half-broken. The stronger, the more potent your sway, so much the freer do I feel from tormenting slavery. Our intercourse will become more and more intimate, and perhaps the goal may be reached before a year has elapsed. Would you, beloved, anticipate the destiny that presides over us, many a sacrifice, many a step, apparently doubtful, might be necessary.' — 'No!' I exclaimed, 'for me nothing will be a sacrifice, no step will appear doubtful to obtain thee entirely. I cannot live longer without thee, I am dying of impatience — of unspeakable pain!' Then Aurora embraced me, and whispered in a scarcely audible voice, 'Art thou happy in my arms?' — 'There is no other happiness,' I exclaimed, and glowing with love even to madness, I pressed the charming creature to my bosom. I felt living kisses upon my lips, and these very kisses were melodies of heaven, through which I heard the words, 'Couldst thou, to possess me, renounce the happiness of an unknown hereafter?' An icy cold shudder trembled through me, but in the midst of this shudder passion raged still more furiously, and I cried in the involuntary madness of love, 'Without thee there is no happiness! — I renounce — '

"I still believe that I stopped here. 'To-morrow night our compact will be concluded,' whispered Aurora, and I felt that she was about to vanish from my arms. I pressed her to me with greater force, she seemed to struggle in vain, when suddenly — I awoke from deep slumber, thinking of the Devil Amor, and the seductive Biondetta. What I had done in that fatal night fell heavily upon my soul. I thought of that unholy invocation by the horrible O'Malley, of the warnings of my pious young friend. I believed that I was in the toils of the evil one — that I was lost. Torn to the very depth of my soul, I sprang up and hastened into the open air. In the street I was met by the major, who held me fast while he said: 'I congratulate you, lieutenant! To tell you the truth, I scarcely gave you credit for so much courage and resolution; you outstrip your master.' Glowing with rage and shame, incapable of uttering a single word, I freed myself from his grasp and pursued my way. The major laughed behind me, and I could detect the scornful laughter of Satan. In the road near those fatal ruins, I perceived a veiled female form, who, lying under a tree, seemed absorbed in a soliloquy. I approached her cautiously, and overheard the words: 'He is mine, he is mine — Oh! bliss of heaven! Even the last trial he has withstood. If men are capable of such love, what is our wretched existence without it?' You may guess that it was Aurora whom I found. She threw back her veil, and love itself cannot be more charming. The delicate paleness of her cheeks, the glance that was sublimed into the sweetest melancholy, made me tremble with unspeakable pleasure. I felt ashamed of my dark thoughts; yet at the very moment when I wished to throw myself at her feet, she had vanished like a form of mist. At the same time I heard a sound in the hedges, as of one clearing one's throat, and out stepped my honest Eulenspiegel, Paul Talkebarth. 'Whence did the devil bring you, fellow?' I began.

"'No, no,' said he, with that queer smile which you know, 'the devil did not bring me here, but very likely he met me. You went out so early, gracious lieutenant, and had forgotten your pipe and tobacco, and I thought so early in the morning, in the damp air — for my aunt at Genthin used to say —'

"'Hold your tongue, prattle, and give me that,' cried I, as I made him hand me the lighted pipe. Scarcely, however, had we proceeded a few paces, than Paul began again very softly, 'My aunt at Genthin used to say, the Root-mannikin (Wurzelmännlein) was not to be trusted; indeed, such a chap was no better than an incubus or a chezim, and ended by breaking one's heart. Old coffee Lizzy here in the suburbs — ah, gracious sir, you should only see what fine flowers, and men, and animals she can pour out. Man should help himself as he can, my aunt at Genthin used to say. I was yesterday with Lizzy and took her a little fine mocha. One of us has a heart as well as the rest — Becker's Dolly is a pretty thing, but then there is something so odd about her eyes, so salamander-like' —

"'What is that you say, fellow?' I exclaimed, hastily. Paul was silent, but began again in a few seconds: 'Yes, Lizzy is a good woman after all; she said, after she had looked at the coffee grounds, that there was nothing the matter with Dolly, and that the salamander look about the eyes came from cracknel-baking or the dancing-room; but, at the same time, she advised me to remain single, and told me that a certain good gentleman was in great danger. These salamanders,

she said, are the worst sort of things that the devil employs
to lure a poor human soul to destruction, because they have
certain passions—ah, one must only stand firm and keep
God in one's heart—then I myself saw in the coffee grounds
Major O'Malley quite like and natural.'

"I bid the fellow hold his tongue, but you may conceive
the feelings that were awakened in me at this strange discourse of Paul's, whom I suddenly found initiated into my
dark secret, and who so unexpectedly displayed a knowledge of cabalistic matters, for which he was probably in-
debted to the coffee-prophetess. I passed the most uneasy
day I ever had in my life. Paul was not to be got out of
the room all that evening, but was constantly returning and
finding something to do. When it was near midnight, and
he was at last obliged to go, he said softly, as if praying to
himself: 'Bear God in thy heart—think of the salvation of
thy soul—and thou wilt resist the enticements of Satan.'

"I cannot describe the manner—I may almost say, the
fearful manner—in which my soul was moved at these sim-
ple words of my servant. All my endeavours to keep myself
awake were in vain. I fell into that state of confused dreaming, which I could not look upon as natural, but as the operation of some foreign principle. The magical beaming woke
me as usual. Aurora, in the full lustre of supernatural beauty, stood before me, and passionately stretched her arms;
towards me. Nevertheless, Paul's pious words shone in my
soul as if written there with letters of fire. 'Depart, thou seductive birth of hell!' I cried, when the terrible O'Malley,
now of a gigantic stature, rose before me, and piercing me
with eyes, from which an infernal fire was flashing, howled
out: 'Resist not—poor atom of humanity. Thou hast become
ours!' My courage could have withstood the frightful as-
pect of the most hideous spectre, but I lost my senses at the
sight of O'Malley, and fell to the ground.

"A loud report awoke me from this state of stupefaction. I felt myself held by the arms of a man, and struggled with all the force of despair, to free myself. 'Gracious lieutenant, it is I,' said a voice in my ears. It was honest Paul who endeavoured to raise me from the ground. I let him have his own way. He would not at first tell me plainly how all had happened, but he at last assured me, with a mysterious smile, that he knew better to what unholy acquaintance the major had lured me, than I could suspect. The old pious Lizzy had revealed every tiling to him. He had not gone to sleep the night before, but had well loaded his gun, and had watched at the door.

"When he had heard me cry aloud and fall to the ground, he had, although his courage failed him a little, burst open the door and entered. 'There,' he continued in his mad way, 'there stood Major O'Malley before me, as frightful to look upon as in the cup of coffee. He grinned at me hideously, but I did not allow myself to be stirred from my purpose and said: "If, gracious major, you are the devil, pardon me for stepping boldly up to you as a pious Christian and saying to you: 'Avaunt, thou cursed Satan-Major, I command thee in the name of the Lord. Begone, or I will fire!'" The major would not give way, but kept on grinning at me, and began to abuse me. I then cried, "Shall I fire? — shall I fire?" and when he persisted in keeping his place I fired in reality. But all had vanished — both Major Satan and Mam'sell Belzebub had departed through the wall!'

"The continued strain upon the mind during the period that had just passed, together with the last frightful moments, threw me upon a tedious sick-bed. When I recovered I left Potsdam, without seeing any more of O'Malley, whose further fate has remained unknown to me. The image of those portentous days grew fainter and fainter, and at last vanished all together, so that I recovered perfect freedom of mind, until here — "

"Well," asked Albert, with the greatest curiosity and astonishment, "do you mean to say you have lost your freedom again here? I cannot conceive, why here—"

"Oh," said Victor, interrupting his friend, while his tone became somewhat solemn, "I can explain all in two words. In the sleepless nights of the illness I endured here, all the dreams of that noblest and most terrible period of my life were revived. It was my glowing passion itself, that assumed a form—Aurora—she again appeared to me—glorified—purified in the fire of Heaven;—no devilish O'Malley has further power over her—Aurora is—the baroness!"

"How! what!" cried Albert, shrinking with horror. Then he muttered to himself, "The little plump housewife with the great bunch of keys—she an elementary spirit!—she a salamander!"—and he felt a difficulty in suppressing his laughter.

"In the figure," continued Victor, "there is no longer any trace of resemblance to be found, that is to say, in ordinary life; but the mysterious fire that flashes from her eyes,—the pressure of her hand."—

"You have been very ill," said Albert, gravely, "for the wound you received in your head was serious enough to put your life in peril; but now I find you are so far recovered that you will be able to go with me. From the very bottom of my heart I implore you, my dear,—my beloved friend, to leave this place, and accompany me to-morrow to Aix-la-Chapelle."

"I certainly do not intend to remain here any longer," replied Victor, "so I will go with you; however, let this matter first be cleared up."

The next morning, when Albert woke, Victor told him that a strange, ghostly sort of dream had revealed to him the mysterious word, which O'Malley had taught him, when they prepared the Teraphim. He thought that he would make use of it for the last time. Albert shook his head doubtfully, and caused every thing to be got ready for a speedy departure, while Paul Talkebarth evinced the most joyful activity by all sorts of mad expressions. "Zackermanthö," he muttered to himself in Albert's hearing. "It is a good thing that the devil Bear fetched the Irish devil Foot long ago, otherwise there would have been something wrong now."

Victor, as he had wished, found the baroness alone in her room, occupied with some domestic work. He told her that he was now at last about to quit the house, where he had enjoyed such noble hospitality. The baroness assured him that she had never entertained a friend more dear to her. Victor then took her hand, and asked her if she were ever at Potsdam, and knew a certain Irish Major. "Victor," said the baroness interrupting him hastily, "we shall part to-day, we shall never see each other again; nay, we must not. A dark veil hangs over my life. Let it suffice if I tell you that a fearful destiny condemns me always to appear a different being from the one which I really am. In the hateful position in which you have found me, and which causes me spiritual torments, which my bodily health seems to belie, I am atoning for a heavy fault—yet no more—farewell!" Upon this, Victor cried with a loud voice: "Nehelmiahmiheal!" and the baroness, with a shriek of horror, fell senseless to the ground. Victor under the influence of a storm of strange feelings, and quite beside himself could scarcely summon resolution enough to ring the bell. However, having done this, he rushed from the chamber. "At once,—let us leave at once!" he cried to his friend, and told him in a few words what had happened. Both leaped upon the horses that had been brought for them, and rode off without waiting for the return of the baron, who had gone out hunting.

Albert's reflections on the ride from Liège to Aix-la-Chapelle have already shown, with what profound earnestness, with what noble feeling, he had appreciated the events of that fatal period. On the journey to the Residence, whither the two friends now returned, he succeeded in completely delivering Victor from the dreamy condition into which he had sunk, and while Albert brought to his friend's mind, depicted in the most lively colours, all the monstrous occurrences which the days of the last campaign had brought forth, the latter felt himself animated by the same spirit as that which dwelt in Albert. And although Albert never ventured upon long contradictions or doubts, Victor himself now seemed to look upon his mystical adventure, as nothing but a bad dream.

In the Residence it was natural that the ladies were favourably disposed to the colonel, who was rich, of noble figure, young for the high rank which he held, and who, moreover, was amiability itself. Albert looked upon him as a lucky man, who might choose the fairest for a wife, but Victor observed, very seriously: "Whether it was, that I had been mystified, and, by wicked means, made to serve some unknown end, or whether an evil power really tried to tempt me, this much is certain, that though the past has not cost me my happiness, it has deprived me of the paradise of love. Never can that time return, when I felt the highest earthly felicity, when the ideal of my sweetest, most transporting dreams, nay, love itself, was in my arms. Love and pleasure have vanished, since a horrible mystery deprived me of her, who to my inmost heart was really a higher being, such as I shall not again find upon earth!"

The colonel remained unmarried.

Books published by Mondial

French Classics:

1. Rougon-Macquart Series:

Emile Zola: The Fortune of the Rougons
ISBN 1595690107 / 9781595690104

Emile Zola: The Fat and the Thin (The Belly of Paris)
ISBN 1595690522 / 9781595690524

Emile Zola: Abbe Mouret's Transgression
(The Sin of the Abbé Mouret) ISBN 1595690506 / 9781595690500

Emile Zola: The Dream. ISBN 1595690492 / 9781595690494

Emile Zola: A Love Episode (A Page of Love)
ISBN 1595690271 / 9781595690272

Emile Zola: The Conquest of Plassans
ISBN 1595690484 / 9781595690487

Emile Zola: The Joy of Life (Zest for Life)
ISBN 1595690476 / ISBN 9781595690470

Emile Zola: Doctor Pascal. ISBN 1595690514 / 9781595690517

Emile Zola: His Excellency (His Excellency, Eugène Rougon)
ISBN 1595690557 / 9781595690555

Emile Zola: Money. ISBN 9781595690630

Emile Zola: The Soil (The Earth). ISBN 9781595690883

Emile Zola: The Downfall (La Debacle). ISBN 9781595691118

2. Other French Literature:

Emile Zola: The Mysteries of Marseille. ISBN 9781595690913

Emile Zola: The Flood. ISBN 9781595690944

Emile Zola: Death. ISBN 9781595690937

Emile Zola: Fruitfulness (The Four Gospels)
ISBN 1595690182 / 9781595690180

Emile Zola: The Fête in Coqueville
(The Coqueville Spree) ISBN 9781595690869

Victor Hugo: Ninety-Three. ISBN 9781595690920

Victor Hugo: Bug-Jargal. ISBN 9781595690951

Victor Hugo: The Man Who Laughs (By Order of the King)
ISBN 1595690131 / 9781595690135

Victor Hugo: History of a Crime. ISBN 1595690204 / 9781595690203

Voltaire: The Princess of Babylon. ISBN 9781595690999

Honoré de Balzac: Ursula (Ursule Mirouet)
ISBN 1595690530 / 9781595690531

Honoré de Balzac: Maitre Cornelius.
ISBN 1595690174 / 9781595690173

Anatole France: Penguin Island. ISBN 1595690298 / 9781595690296

Anatole France: The Crime of Sylvestre Bonnard
ISBN 9781595690593

Gustave Flaubert: Salammbo (Salambo)
ISBN 1595690352 / 9781595690357

Romain Rolland: Pierre and Luce . ISBN 9781595690609

Jules Verne: An Antarctic Mystery (The Sphinx of the Ice Fields)
ISBN 1595690549 / 9781595690548

André Gide: Strait is the Gate. (La Porte étroite) ISBN 9781595690623

André Gide: Prometheus Illbound. ISBN 9781595690807

André Gide: Recollections of Oscar Wilde. ISBN 9781595690814

Alphonse Daudet:
Little What's-His-Name (aka Little Good-for-Nothing)
(Le Petit Chose. French Classics) ISBN 9781595691057

German Classics:

Heinrich Heine: Germany. A Winter Tale (Deutschland. Ein Wintermärchen.) Bilingual Edition. ISBN 9781595690715

Heinrich Heine: The Rabbi of Bacharach
(German Classics) ISBN 9781595691002

Heinrich Heine: Florentine Nights.
(German Classics) ISBN 9781595691019

Heinrich Heine: From the Memoirs of Herr von Schnabelewopski
(German Classics) ISBN 9781595691026

Johann Wolfgang von Goethe: The Sorrows of Young Werther
ISBN 159569045X / 9781595690456

Theodor Storm: The Rider of the White Horse
(The Dikegrave; aka The Dykemaster) ISBN 9781595690746

Heinrich von Kleist: Michael Kohlhaas (A Tale from an Old Chronicle)
ISBN 9781595690760

Gottfried Keller: A Village Romeo and Juliet
(Swiss-German Classics) ISBN 9781595690791

Gottfried Keller: Ursula (Swiss-German Classics). ISBN 9781595690838

Gottfried Keller: The Governor of Greifensee
(Swiss-German Classics) ISBN 9781595690845

Wilhelm Raabe: The Hunger Pastor
(German Classics) ISBN 9781595690753

Theodor Storm, Adelbert von Chamisso, Adalbert Stifter: Famous
German Novellas of the 19th Century (Immensee. Peter Schlemihl.
Brigitta.) ISBN 159569014X / 9781595690142

Franz Grillparzer: The Poor Musician. ISBN 9781595691095

Marie von Ebner-Eschenbach: Krambambuli. The District Doctor
(Two Novellas. German Classics). ISBN 9781595691040

E. T. A. Hoffmann: The Sandman. The Elementary Spirit
(Two Tales. German Classics). ISBN 9781595691170

Wilhelm Hauff: The Cold Heart. Nose, the Dwarf
(Two Tales. German Classics). ISBN 9781595691187

Other books:

Agatha Christie: Two Novels (The Mysterious Affair at Styles.
The Secret Adversary.) ISBN 1595690417 / 9781595690418

Jack London: War of the Classes. Revolution. The Shrinkage of the
Planet. ISBN 1595690409 / 9781595690401

Jack London: Before Adam. Children of the Frost.
ISBN 1595690395 / 9781595690395

Jack London: The Iron Heel. ISBN 1595690379 / 9781595690371

Jack London: Burning Daylight. ISBN 9781595691064

Oscar Wilde: The Critic as Artist. Upon the Importance of Doing
Nothing and Discussing Everything. ISBN 9781595690821

Oscar Wilde, Anonymous: Teleny
or The Reverse of the Medal (Gay erotic classic)
ISBN 1595690360 / 9781595690364

Martin Andersen Nexo: Pelle the Conqueror (Complete Edition: Boyhood. Apprenticeship. The Great Struggle. Daybreak.) ISBN 159569028X / 9781595690289

Martin Andersen Nexo: Ditte Everywoman (Complete Edition: Girl Alive. Daughter of Man. Towards the Stars.) ISBN 9781595690333

Susan Coolidge: Clover. ISBN 1595690263 / 9781595690265

Jerome K. Jerome: Idle Thoughts of an Idle Fellow ISBN 1595690247 / 9781595690241

Malama Katulwende: Bitterness (An African Novel from Zambia) ISBN 159569031X / 9781595690319

Sigmund Freud: Dream Psychology (Psychoanalysis for Beginners) ISBN 1595690166 / 9781595690166

Gertrude Stein: Three Lives (With an Introduction by Carl Van Vechten). ISBN 1595690425 / 9781595690425

Virgina Woolf: Jacob's Room. ISBN 9781595691149

Jane Austen: Persuasion. Northanger Abbey (Two Novels) ISBN: 9781595691156

Sinclair Lewis: The Trail of the Hawk. ISBN 9781595691132

William Somerset Maugham: The Trembling of a Leaf ISBN 9781595691194

Gabriele D'Annunzio:
The Child of Pleasure. ISBN 9781595690581

Luigi Pirandello: Signora Speranza. ISBN 9781595691088:

Carl Van Vechten: Firecrackers.
A Realistic Novel. ISBN 9781595690685

Bruce Kellner: Winter Ridge. A Love Story. ISBN 9781595690692

Donald Windham: Two People (Gay Classics). ISBN 9781595691033

Frederick (Friedrich) Engels: Socialism: Utopian and Scientific (Appendix: The Mark; Preface by Karl Marx) ISBN 1595690468 / 9781595690463

Karl Marx: The Eighteenth Brumaire of Louis Bonaparte. ISBN 1595690239 / 9781595690234